Anna Mei, Blessing in Disguise

Read all of Anna Mei's adventures . . .

Anna Mei, Cartoon Girl

Anna Mei, Escape Artist

Anna Mei, Blessing in Disguise

Anna Mei
Blessing in Disguise

By Carol A. Grund

Pauline
BOOKS & MEDIA
Boston

Library of Congress Cataloging-in-Publication Data

Grund, Carol A.

  Anna Mei, blessing in disguise / by Carol A. Grund.

     p. cm.

Sequel to: Anna Mei, escape artist.

  Summary: Twelve-year-old Anna Mei is settled into her Michigan home and happy to start seventh grade at Westside Junior High with her friends, but a new boy in town causes her to revisit her feelings about her own identity and Chinese heritage.

  ISBN 0-8198-0796-6 (pbk.)

[1. Identity--Fiction. 2. Chinese Americans--Fiction. 3. Junior high schools--Fiction. 4. Schools--Fiction. 5. Family life--Michigan--Fiction. 6. Science fairs--Fiction. 7. Adoption--Fiction. 8. Michigan--Fiction.] I. Title.

  PZ7.G9328Anm 2011

  [Fic]--dc22

                           2011008784

Many manufacturers and sellers distinguish their products through the use of trademarks. Any trademarked designations that appear in this book are used in good faith but are not authorized by, associated with, or sponsored by the trademark owners.

Cover art by Wayne Alfano

Design by Mary Joseph Peterson, FSP

"Book Guides: Investigating Anna Mei" by Kimberly A. Grotbeck

"P" and PAULINE are registered trademarks of the Daughters of St. Paul.

Published by Pauline Books & Media, 50 Saint Pauls Avenue, Boston, MA 02130-3491

Printed in U.S.A.

AMBD VSAUSAPEOILL6-1J11-03806 0796-6

www.pauline.org

Pauline Books & Media is the publishing house of the Daughters of St. Paul, an international congregation of women religious serving the Church with the communications media.

1 2 3 4 5 6 7 8 9   13 12 11

Bringing Anna Mei's story to life has been a journey filled with blessings.

I'm grateful to everyone at Pauline Books & Media, who took a leap of faith by embracing the series and its novice author. Their kindness and support have lighted every step of the way.

Special thanks to my editor, Jaymie, who planted the seed for this third story and then nurtured it with tender loving care. Her talented, steadfast guidance, along with her devotion to her own daughter Juliana, inspired me to bring Anna Mei's story to a place I could be proud of.

✳

Finally, to my family, friends, and all the readers who have joined me on the journey—no one ever had better traveling companions. My heart is full.

Contents

Chapter One

Werewolf at the Door

When the werewolf appeared at her bedroom door, Anna Mei Anderson was sitting in her green-striped chair, just starting some math homework. In a horror movie, the situation would have called for some terrified screaming, maybe even a daring escape out the second-story window.

In real life, Anna Mei just shook her head, smiling.

"Hi Dad," she said. "Been going through the Halloween box again?"

Snapping and snarling, he came in and looked at himself in her mirror. "I've already worn all of those," he said, his voice muffled behind all the fake fur and latex. "I wanted something new this year, so I stopped at the costume shop on my way home. What do you think?"

"I think I agree with Mom—when it comes to Halloween, some people never grow up."

Her father peeled off the mask, making his hair stand practically straight up. Lately Anna Mei had started to notice strands of silver mixed in with the blond. Even though she knew he turned forty-six on his last birthday, it seemed weird to think of her father as getting older. To her he always looked the same—tall and thin, with a dent on his nose where his dark-rimmed glasses sat, and a crooked smile that reached all the way up to his blue eyes.

Now he patted his hair down and put his glasses back on. When he turned away from the mirror, he looked like the mild-mannered research scientist that he actually was.

"When it comes to Halloween," he said, "I think *everyone* should get to be a kid. Which brings me to my next question—what about you? Have you decided on a costume yet?"

"Honestly, Dad, I've been so busy since school started," she told him, "I haven't had time to think about it."

"Lots of homework this year, huh?" he asked, looking at the big pile of textbooks she'd dumped onto the bed.

"Well, yeah," she answered, "but that's only part of it. I also have volleyball almost every day, and Science Club every week, plus hanging out with my friends. It all takes time."

"I noticed," he said. "If you get any busier, your mom and I are going to start renting out your room. *Someone* might as well be using it."

"Okay, I don't think it's quite that—*oof!*"

Her cat, who had scooted under the bed when the snarling werewolf appeared, picked that moment to launch herself into Anna Mei's lap, knocking her math book to the floor.

"Have you been listening, Cleo?" Anna Mei said, ruffling the cat's grey and white fur. "I have a feeling you don't like the idea of someone else taking over my room."

Her father reached down to retrieve the book. "Either that or she's courageously trying to save you from death by algebra," he suggested.

As he added that book to the pile on her bed, another one caught his attention. "Wow, this one's huge!" he said, picking it up and hefting it. "It must weigh at least five pounds."

"Tell me about it," she said. "That's social studies. And Mr. Crandall gives homework almost every night."

"*Studies in Culture: Africa, Asia, and Australia,*" Dad read aloud from the cover. "That sounds interesting."

Anna Mei had learned a long time ago that *interesting* often meant something completely different to adults than it did to her. "I guess," she said, shrugging.

"I always wished your mom and I could have seen more of China when we were there," he said, looking through the book for the Asian section. "It's so big— we barely had time to scratch the surface."

Twelve years ago, Anna Mei had been born in Hunan, a province in southern China. She didn't remember it, of course—she had been only six months old when the Andersons adopted her from the orphanage and brought her home with them to Boston. Growing up there, she had rarely given any thought to the fact that her life began somewhere else.

That is, until a year ago, when the three of them moved to Michigan. Suddenly she seemed to stick out like a sore thumb—the new girl who was Chinese and, oh by the way, her parents weren't.

At first she worked pretty hard to prove that she was just like everyone else. But when her sixth grade social studies teacher assigned a class project on heritage, Anna Mei decided to go ahead and tell the class about her birth country. She did some research about the city of Yiyang, where the orphanage was. And she showed them the note her birth mother had pinned to her baby clothes, calling her "Mei Li"— beautiful plum blossom.

After that, she was relieved when no one treated her any differently than before. It turned out that where you were born or what your family looked like wasn't a big deal to most people. But now her father, looking at a map of Asia in her social studies book, seemed to expect her to be excited about studying China, a place almost as foreign to her as Africa or Australia.

"Well, you'll have to get back to me when you get to that section," he said, "assuming you can find a few minutes to spare for your old dad."

"Hey, it's not like I'm the only busy one around here," she pointed out. "You've been working late almost every night, even on Mom's nights at the hospital. Zandra's parents are the ones bringing me home from volleyball."

"You've got a point there," he admitted. "This project I'm working on is pretty intense. The good news is that the university has promised to hire a consultant, so I'll be getting some help soon."

"It's about time," she said, and knew it sounded grumpy. But she was still ticked off that his project was the reason the family never got to take a trip to Boston over the summer. She had been looking forward to seeing her old friends again, especially Lauren, and going to the places where they used to hang out. That trip had been postponed until her father could manage to get away from the lab.

"Speaking of time," he said, putting the book back down on the bed, "it's getting late. There's either a real werewolf hiding in here somewhere, or my stomach is growling for dinner. How does spaghetti sound?"

"Like this," she told him, sucking in her cheeks and slurping loudly.

He laughed, as she knew he would. The cornier the joke, the more he liked it.

"Okay, give me about twenty minutes," he said, heading out the door. Then he stopped and stuck his head back in. "And start thinking about a costume. Only two weeks left, you know."

She had to smile. It was like he still thought of her as a little kid, getting all excited about going trick-or-treating on Halloween. She would be thirteen in January—he was going to have to notice her growing up sooner or later.

"I will," she promised, then moved a protesting Cleo off her lap so she could get back to her math homework.

Chapter Two

Fifth Period Lunch

A week later, Anna Mei stood at her locker, trying to hurry as she twisted the dial on her combination lock. Her lunch period was starting, and she wanted to spend as much of it as possible with her friends.

Westside Junior High combined all the seventh and eighth graders from the three elementary schools in town, totaling about 400 students. It was smaller than the middle school Anna Mei would have gone to in Boston, but she still thought of it as a step up. She liked being in a place where everyone was around her age. She liked changing classes every fifty minutes, rotating through the school, and having a different teacher for each subject. And given the number of books she was expected to lug around, she liked having a locker to stash them in.

Because lockers were assigned alphabetically, hers was locker number three, right between Martin Alvarez and Maddie Armstrong. Neither of them was here at the moment—they both had fourth period lunch. Anna Mei had that one, too, on Mondays, Wednesdays, and Fridays. But on Tuesdays and Thursdays she had an elective class in the morning that bumped her lunch to fifth period.

Thank goodness for Spanish class, she thought, shoving her books into her locker and grabbing her lunch bag.

Not that it was her favorite class—not even close—but taking Spanish twice a week meant she could have lunch with all three of her best friends. So far, that was the biggest drawback to life at Westside. After being in the same sixth-grade class at Elmwood Elementary, and then hanging out over the summer, the four of them had been excited about going to junior high together. And although they shared a few of the same classes, Anna Mei missed being able to see them all day long.

At least she and Zandra had matching lunch periods every day. On the days Anna Mei was in Spanish class, Zandra had choir. And since her last name was Caine, her locker was just down the hall from Anna Mei's. The two girls headed for the cafeteria together, where today they found Danny Gallagher and Luis Hernandez already at their usual table.

Luis looked up and saw them coming. "*Hola, mis amigas*," he said. As they sat down, he turned to Anna Mei with a smile. "*¿Y cómo estás hoy?*"

He had grown up speaking Spanish, and now that Anna Mei was studying it, he liked to use it on her. Luckily, "*cómo estás*" was an easy one.

"*Muy bien*," she answered. "I'm fine. *Gracias*."

"That's *muy* impressive," Danny told them both. "But for the sake of the non-Spanish speakers sitting here, would you mind switching to English?"

"Okay," Luis agreed, grinning. "As long as *you* promise not to pull out the old 'sure and begorrah' stuff."

Danny looked as Irish as he was, with a wide smile to go with his red hair and freckles. Over the summer he'd gotten taller, Anna Mei noticed. And he was planning to join the swim team next semester, so he'd started exercising more and eating healthier. He still pretty much inhaled his lunch, but at least now it had more fruits and vegetables in it.

Zandra laughed as she took a sandwich and banana out of her lunch bag. "I'd be nice to them if I were you, Danny," she said. "Aren't you taking Spanish next semester?"

"Oh yeah," he said, polishing an apple on his shirt sleeve. "What I meant to say was, feel free to practice all the Spanish you want, *por favor*."

"Not today, though," Anna Mei said. "We don't

have much time, and I don't even know the Spanish word for what I want to talk about."

"Which is—?" Zandra prompted, pulling the lid off her yogurt container.

"Halloween," Anna Mei said. "It's coming up on Sunday, so we need to start making our plans now."

Danny groaned as he picked up his milk carton. "There she goes again, planning everything to within an inch of its life."

"Well, Danny," she said, with a deep sigh, "feel free to wait until five o'clock on Halloween night to decide what you want to do. There might still be time to draw a face on a paper bag and wear it over your head."

She figured he would have some kind of sarcastic comeback, but it was Luis who spoke first.

"Something tells me it wouldn't be the first time," he said.

In the next moment they were all laughing—including Danny. And luckily for the rest of them, he managed to swallow his mouthful of milk first.

Chapter Three

Friends Like These

As she looked around the table, Anna Mei wished she could take a picture of this moment—four friends, joking around, having fun, making plans to spend time together. It seemed impossible that only a year ago she had barely known them.

After those first confusing months, she had stopped struggling against the idea of having to leave Boston and find a new life here. And as soon as she stopped worrying about fitting in and finding some friends, they found her.

I'm so lucky, Anna Mei thought. *With friends like these, seventh grade is going to be my best year ever.*

They spent the rest of the lunch period talking about the upcoming weekend. Zandra and Luis both had younger brothers and sisters who went to

Elmwood, so they were going to the school carnival with their families on Friday night. That gave Anna Mei an idea. "My cousin Emily is in first grade at Pinewood," she said. "I'll ask my aunt if I can take her to the carnival. We could all meet up there."

"What about me?" Danny asked. "Do I have to rent a kid in order to get in?"

Anna Mei laughed. Danny's only sibling was his brother Connor, a six-footer who played linebacker on the high school football team. "Don't worry," she said. "I'll share Emily with you. She'll get a kick out of seeing all the other kids in their costumes."

"R.J. wants to be a pirate," Zandra reported. "But Marcus has come up with at least ten different ideas so far. My mom's threatening to just dress him in his Spiderman pajamas and call it good."

By the time the bell rang, they had all agreed to meet at the carnival on Friday night, and then get together at Anna Mei's on Saturday for pizza and movies. They ran out of time before they could talk about Halloween, but that was okay—whatever they decided to do, she knew it would be fun.

On Friday, Anna Mei's father waited in the car while she walked up to the Gallaghers' house and rang the doorbell. A moment later Danny appeared, dressed in jeans and a zip-up sweatshirt.

"Sorry," he said, "you're a little early for trick-or-treating. Come back in a few days and I'll see what I can do."

"Very funny. I thought I'd say hello to your parents before we go."

"They're not here," he said. "They decided to go to Connor's game in Brighton. Come on in while I grab my key."

She waited in the front hallway while Danny got a set of keys from the kitchen. "All set," he said. "Let's go."

"But . . . aren't you forgetting something?" she asked.

"I don't think so," he said. "All I need is a couple of bucks for some food and games, right?"

"I mean your costume," Anna Mei said. "We all agreed to wear one, remember?"

It was hard to keep the disappointment out of her voice. Last year, Danny came to the carnival dressed as a mad scientist, wearing a lab coat he'd borrowed from her father. The creative touches he'd added—featuring green slime and purple hairspray—had made it a very memorable outfit.

She had to admit that her own costume this year had been a little last-minute. After promising her father she'd think about it, she came up with a vague idea of doing something with moons and stars, maybe going as the Milky Way. But when she called to invite Emily to the carnival, she found out that her cousin would be dressed as a butterfly. Inspired at last, Anna Mei quickly pulled together some cargo pants, a khaki shirt and a pair of hiking boots. Then she found a plastic pith helmet in the Halloween box, grabbed her old butterfly net from the garage and *voilà*—instant butterfly catcher.

It might not be as creative as some of her previous costumes, but at least she'd tried. What was Danny's excuse?

"Don't worry," he assured her, patting the pocket of his sweatshirt. "My costume is right in here."

She looked at him suspiciously. "Why do I get the feeling you're up to something?"

"Because you're cynical by nature, that's why," he said. "Not only do I have an actual costume, I predict it will be the best one at the carnival. Look—I'll prove it."

He unzipped his sweatshirt to reveal a sign pinned to his shirt. In fancy lettering it said "Bless You." Then he reached into his sweatshirt pocket and pulled out a pair of plastic glasses, the kind with a big fake nose, fuzzy eyebrows, and a black moustache attached.

With the glasses on, he opened his arms dramatically. "Ta da!"

She frowned, still feeling let down. "Okay, I give up, what are you supposed to be?"

"Come on, isn't it *obvious*?" he asked. "I'm a blessing . . . in disguise."

She stared at him, trying to process it.

Then she burst out laughing. Who else but Danny Gallagher would come up with an idea like that? No one, that's who, and that's why there was no one she would rather be going to the carnival with tonight.

"Okay, I admit it," she said, when she could breathe again. "It's the perfect costume, especially for you."

He grinned as they stepped out onto the porch. "Let's go show your dad," he said, locking the door behind him. "Do you think he'll like it?"

She was still laughing as they headed for the car. "Isn't it *obvious*?" she asked.

Chapter Four

Jack-o-Lantern Genius

On Saturday, Anna Mei's friends gathered in her kitchen, carving pumpkins while they waited for Mr. Anderson's homemade pizza to come out of the oven. The table was covered in newspaper, while the newspaper was covered in what Danny called "pumpkin guts."

"Hey, Danny, quit hogging the scraper," Luis said. "You've had it for the last twenty minutes."

"Clearly you've never learned the secret to carving a great jack-o-lantern," Danny told him. "You have to get the shell nice and thin before you start cutting."

Zandra laughed. "And all this time I thought the secret was the ability to cut triangles."

"Triangles?" Danny practically snorted. Then, shaking his head, "Amateurs."

By the time the pizza was ready, the mess was safely in the trash can and four jack-o-lanterns were lined up on the countertop. They all looked pretty good, Anna Mei thought, but Danny's creation was a true work of art, featuring a fire-breathing dragon that wrapped around the pumpkin in one long curve. Lit up at night, it would be spectacular.

"I've never seen anything like it," Anna Mei's father said. "You're a jack-o-lantern genius."

Danny blushed all the way up to his red hair. "It's not that big of a deal," he said. "People are good at all different things. I . . . draw."

"That's like saying Mozart played piano," Dad said, grinning. "But for now let's get these guys moved to the patio so I can present my own masterpiece. In other words, dinner is served."

A few minutes later they were all enjoying veggie pizza with homemade tomato sauce, along with chips and salsa from Luis's uncle's restaurant.

"This is really good, Mr. Anderson," Zandra said. "Way better than pepperoni."

"I'm glad you like it," Dad said. "I'm a pretty big fan of vegetables myself. After all, plants help put food on this table."

"You trained your plants to set the table?" Danny asked, reaching for another slice of pizza.

Anna Mei groaned but Mom laughed. "He means his job, Danny. He gets paid to work with plants."

"Well, I like to think it's a little more glamorous than *that*," Dad said, spooning out more salsa. "After all, I work with one of the largest groups of plant biochemists in North America."

"What exactly does a plant biochemist do, Mr. Anderson?" Luis asked. "It's not a job kids dream about, like being a firefighter or a pilot."

"Well, they should—studying the molecular and cellular structures of plants is fascinating," Dad said, his eyes shining brightly behind his glasses. "For example, right now my team is researching the regulation of metabolic processes by environmental factors—things like cold temperatures, phosphate deprivation, or bacterial pathogens."

Danny grinned. "Exactly what I was going to say, Mr. A."

"Okay, I know it sounds complicated," Dad said, smiling, "but what it boils down to is finding ways to nurture and protect plants, for the good of the whole planet. With enough research, maybe we can improve nutrition for people around the world, or find a way to replace fossil fuels. I can't think of any work that's more important—or more exciting."

"Now do you see why I'm such a Science geek?" Anna Mei asked. "It's obviously . . . hereditary."

They seemed to let this sink in for a moment. Then everyone laughed, including her.

Being adopted really isn't a big deal, she thought, reaching for the water pitcher and refilling her glass. *I can even joke about it, and no one thinks it's weird.*

"I just wish you were old enough to be my lab assistant," her father said. "Then maybe I could get a little time off now and then."

Mom brought over a pan of brownies she'd left cooling on the counter. "Didn't you say they were bringing in some help for you?"

"That's true," Dad said. "We're partnering with The Great Lakes Bioenergy Research Center, and they've hired a temporary consultant to help out. From what I understand, his wife and son are coming, too."

"Really? Where are they from?" Mom asked.

"Originally from Beijing, I believe," Dad said. "But Dr. Chen is very experienced, so I would guess they've lived in quite a few places by now."

"That sounds cool," Danny said. "I've never been anywhere more exotic than Indiana!"

Dad smiled. "I think their son is a bit younger than all of you, though. Which reminds me, Anna Mei, once the Chens arrive, I'll be counting on you to spend some time with him. I'd like him to feel that he has at least one friend here."

The bite of brownie Anna Mei was chewing suddenly felt dry.

He doesn't mean anything by it, she thought, forcing herself to swallow. *It's not because I'm Chinese. He'd want me to be nice to these people no matter where they were from.*

Everyone seemed to have stopped talking, waiting for her answer. She cleared her throat. "Sure," she said. "Maybe we could introduce him to Zandra's brothers."

Zandra laughed. "Great idea, Anna Mei. Marcus and R.J. will have him knocking things over and falling out of trees in no time."

Chapter Five

All Stressed Out

S cience Club met after school on Wednesdays. The moderator, Miss Haynes, also taught seventh grade science.

"I hope you'll all consider joining," she said to her students on the first day of school. "The only requirement is a fascination with the natural world around us."

That's me, Anna Mei thought. It would be hard to squeeze in, with volleyball practice three days a week, plus games. But how could she pass up a chance to do something she loved, with other kids who loved it, too?

She hadn't been able to convince Zandra, Danny, or Luis to sign up, but at least a dozen other seventh graders joined, including a handful of girls. Miss

Haynes explained that the main purpose of the club was to prepare for Science Quest. Teams from middle schools and high schools across the country competed in this event each year, with the top teams advancing from regional to state to national levels. Along the way, hundreds of certificates, medals, trophies and scholarships were awarded.

Anna Mei couldn't wait to get started—she could already picture herself helping to present a project in Washington, D.C., the site of this year's finals. A couple of months into the semester, she was still excited about the club. But for the first time, she wished she didn't have a meeting today.

Sitting in social studies, the last class of the day, she was so tired she could barely keep her eyes open. She'd stayed up late on Saturday night watching movies with her friends. Then on Sunday she went trick-or-treating with Zandra and her brothers and sister. After that she still had homework to do.

Then there was volleyball. They were nearing the end of the season, but tournaments would be starting soon. Teams that won at the local level would advance to regionals, which meant traveling out of town for more games.

Just thinking about it made her head feel heavy. If only she could close her eyes for a few minutes, maybe that would—

"Anna Mei?"

Her eyes snapped open. Her teacher, Mr. Crandall, was standing next to her desk. "Are we boring you?" he asked.

A few of the kids laughed. Anna Mei could feel her cheeks growing warm. "Sorry, Mr. Crandall. I just . . . have a headache today."

"Do you need to see the school nurse?"

"No, I'm okay. Sorry," she said again, hoping he would give her a break and just move on.

"We've been talking about Nigeria," he said, not moving anywhere. "Can you name one of the countries that borders it?"

At that moment Anna Mei wasn't sure she could name a country that bordered *this* one. She struggled to picture the map of western Africa from last night's reading assignment. She remembered opening the book as soon as she got home from practice, but then Dad had called to say he would be late getting home, and Aunt Karen had called to ask if she could come over and babysit for a few hours on Saturday, and Zandra had—

Zandra.

"Cameroon," Anna Mei said. Now she clearly remembered thinking about Zandra while she read her social studies book last night. In Zandra's heritage report last year, she had described how her ancestors lived in Cameroon before the slave traders came.

"Good," Mr. Crandall said. "Cameroon borders the east side of Nigeria. One of its most unique features is that it has beaches, deserts, mountains, rainforests, and savannas, all within its borders. Can you tell us what—"

Mercifully the bell rang at that moment, and Mr. Crandall finally moved toward the front of the room. "Remember, your answers to the questions at the end of chapter nine are due tomorrow," he said, raising his voice over the noise of twenty-six students grabbing their backpacks and heading for the door.

Danny, who'd been sitting a few rows behind her, walked with Anna Mei toward the seventh grade hallway.

"Are you okay?" he asked. "For a minute there it looked like you didn't know the answer. I thought I was in an alternate universe or something."

She smiled. "Are you calling me a know-it-all?"

"Let's just say it's pretty unusual for you not to be on top of things."

"I'm really tired lately," she admitted, yawning even as the words came out of her mouth. "There's just so much to do."

They stopped at Danny's locker, standing their ground as an avalanche of kids rushed past them in a mad dash for the exits.

"I know we joked about being seventh grade superheroes," he said, twisting the dial on his lock. "But even superheroes can only do so much before they flame out."

She frowned. What was that supposed to mean? "So . . . you're saying I shouldn't be doing volleyball and Science Club and homework?"

"No, I'm saying that sometimes you get too stressed out about things. It's okay to not always be first or fastest or best at everything. In other words," he flashed that trademark Danny Gallagher grin, "give yourself a break, Cartoon Girl."

His words managed to squeeze past the headache fogging up her brain. Danny had a way of cutting right to the chase. And he had used his old nickname for her, the one he called her on the first day they met. He told her later it was because her name sounded like *anime*, a Japanese cartoon style, and he was a huge fan of cartoons. He still used it once in a while when he really wanted to get her attention.

She let out a long breath. "So tell me something, Danny—if I'm supposed to be the smart one, how come you always have all the answers?"

He grinned at her as he slammed his locker shut. "It's a gift."

Chapter Six

The Odd One Out

By the end of the week Anna Mei felt better. Skipping the Science Club meeting and a volleyball practice gave her time to catch up on sleep and recharge her batteries. Danny was right—she was going to burn out trying to do everything perfectly. Life was better at a little slower pace.

So when her father came home on Friday with the news that the Chen family had arrived and would be coming for dinner on Sunday, she felt up to it.

"I met Dr. Chen at the lab today," Dad said, taking leftover chicken out of the refrigerator for dinner. On Mondays, Wednesdays, and Fridays, Mom worked a noon-to-midnight nursing shift at the hospital.

"They're staying at a hotel for now, but he was asking me for advice about where to rent a house."

"That's kind of funny," Anna Mei said, getting plates and salad bowls out of the cupboard. "I mean, we've only been here for a year, and we don't even live near the university."

"I told him that," Dad said, "but he was still interested in my impressions of the area. He's very concerned about getting his son enrolled in school as soon as possible."

He explained that the son's name was Kai Hao, pronounced like it rhymed with "tie now." And he was eleven years old, which made him a sixth-grader.

"Dr. Chen is very fluent in English, but I'm not sure about Mrs. Chen or Kai."

Anna Mei was already forming a picture of Kai Hao Chen in her mind. The boy who was coming for dinner on Sunday would be shy and unsure. He would struggle to express himself in English, which might mean he would lag behind the other sixth-graders at his new school. He would probably be on the small side, like her. And also like her, he would be self-conscious and worried about making friends.

The least I can do is be friendly to the poor kid, she thought, feeling a wave of sympathy for him. *Maybe if I help him out when he first gets here, he won't have as hard a time as I did.*

"Don't worry, Dad," she said. "I know how it feels to be the new kid. I'll get my friends together, ask him to go to a movie or play video games with us. I'll even help him with homework if he wants."

"That's my girl," Dad said, with a smile.

They went to early Mass on Sunday so Mom could get a roast in the oven. While it was cooking she mixed up a batch of yeast rolls, plus a glaze for the carrots, fretting the whole time that maybe she should have made fish instead.

"Relax, Margaret," Dad assured her, standing at the sink. She'd given him the job of scrubbing a pile of small, red potatoes. "I'm sure it will be delicious."

"I just hope the gravy comes out all right," she said. "That can be kind of tricky, you know."

"It sure smells good, Mom," Anna Mei said, thinking that her parents were making an awfully big deal about this, considering they didn't even know these people.

"Well, it won't be fancy," her mother said. "But they'll get a taste of what a good old-fashioned Sunday dinner is like." To Anna Mei, it sounded like something her mom's own mother would have said. Anna Mei still missed her Grandmother Anna, who had lived near them in Boston but died a few years ago.

By the time the Chens arrived by taxi, promptly at one o'clock, the table was set, extra chairs were in place, and Mom's gravy was warming in a pan.

Anna Mei's father made the introductions. "Dr.

and Mrs. Chen, this is my wife Margaret and my daughter Anna Mei."

Dr. Jinhai Chen was slim and straight, with thinning hair that was a mixture of black and gray. He wore wire-framed glasses and a dark blue suit. Anna Mei guessed that he was about five foot six, much shorter than her own father. He offered a beautifully wrapped bouquet of fresh flowers to her mother.

"These are a small token of our gratitude for your hospitality," he said. "Please allow me to present my wife, Lian Chen."

Mrs. Chen, even shorter than her husband, was also dressed formally, in a navy skirt and jacket over a snow-white blouse. Her dark hair was short and perfectly styled, revealing delicate pearl drop earrings. Although the two women were probably close in age, Anna Mei thought Mrs. Chen looked much older than her own mother, who was dressed in slim gray slacks and a soft cream sweater.

"I am very pleased to meet you," Mrs. Chen said, speaking more haltingly than her husband. She had a strong accent, but a soft voice. "My family is most honored to be welcomed in your home."

The boy had been standing beside his mother but now she nudged him forward. "My son Kai Hao wishes also to extend his greeting."

Anna Mei was surprised to see that although Kai was a year younger than her, he was actually a little taller. His features strongly resembled his father's, except that his hair was still thick and dark, and he didn't wear glasses. Even his dress shirt and striped tie were similar to his father's.

"Mr. Anderson, Mrs. Anderson," Kai said, bowing slightly as he shook their hands in a firm grip, the way his father had. "Thank you for inviting us."

He turned to Anna Mei. "I am happy to meet you, Anna Mei," he said. "My father tells me you were born in southern China. I have visited there many times."

"Oh. Well, I'm not—I don't—I mean, yes I was," she said, feeling herself blush as she stumbled over the words. This wasn't going the way she had pictured it at all. *He* was supposed to be the one struggling to make conversation, the one who felt awkward and unsure. So why, standing in her own living room with her own family, did *she* suddenly feel like the odd one out?

Chapter Seven

Showing Off

She took a breath and started again. "I was raised in Boston, though. On the east coast," she added, in case his grasp of US geography wasn't very strong.

"Oh yes, Boston," he said, nodding, "the capital of Massachusetts. It was founded in the seventeenth century; quite old by American standards. Later it was the site of several important events in the American Revolution."

So much for the language barrier, Anna Mei thought. *Not only is his English perfect, but he sounds like an encyclopedia.*

"Um, right," she said, hearing how completely lame it sounded. But who knew she would need to prepare some witty remarks about the founding of Boston?

Thankfully her mother came to her rescue. "I'll go put these lovely flowers in some water. Please make yourselves comfortable and I'll be right back."

Once they were settled in the living room, Dad turned to Kai. "I wish I could say I knew as much about Beijing as you do about Boston," he said. "I'm very impressed."

Kai's mother beamed at the compliment.

"My son has attended many good schools," Dr. Chen said proudly, "in many parts of the world. Now we are anxious for him to begin a new experience in the midwestern United States. Tomorrow he will take placement tests."

"I'm sure you'll do a great job on those, Kai," Dad said. "There are some very good schools in this area. Are you interested in any clubs or sports?"

Kai's face brightened. "Basketball," he said. "My favorite American players are Kobe Bryant and Dwayne Wade."

"Two of the very best," Dad agreed.

"My father took me to see them play at the Beijing Olympics in 2008."

Dad's voice rose with excitement. "The year the United States won the gold medal? That must have been amazing!"

"Yes, a very interesting experience," Dr. Chen said, "although my knowledge of the sport is far less than my son's. Basketball has only recently become popular in China."

"Do you play, Mr. Anderson?" Kai asked. "You are very tall."

"I used to, quite a lot," Dad said. "I still play an occasional pick-up game at the gym, or shoot around in the driveway with Anna Mei. She's pretty busy with volleyball these days, though."

Then before Anna Mei could stop him, he was telling everyone how good she had gotten since volleyball camp, and how a defensive play she'd made helped win a game last week. The Chens all smiled and nodded, but she guessed they were probably counting the minutes until dinner was ready.

"So, Mom," she jumped in, the minute Dad slowed down to take a breath, "don't you need help checking on the roast or something?"

It wasn't subtle but at least it took the attention off of her and put it back on dinner, where it belonged. Besides, the sooner everyone was eating, the sooner this would all be over.

"I don't get it," Zandra said in the cafeteria on Monday. She had finished her lunch and was waiting for Anna Mei to do the same so they could spend a few minutes outside before the bell rang for afternoon classes.

Anna Mei had been too busy talking to eat. Now she hurriedly took a bite of her tuna sandwich, washing it down with a sip of milk.

"Don't get what?" she asked.

"Well, all you've done is complain about this kid, but I don't see what he did that bugs you so much. He didn't say anything rude, right? Or spend the whole time burping?"

"Of course not," Anna Mei said, laughing. But she knew why Zandra had asked. She'd spent enough mealtimes with the Caine family to know that hearing boys burping at the dinner table wasn't exactly a rare event. "It's just the opposite. He was all, 'So pleased to make your acquaintance.' He kept calling my dad 'sir,' and he pulled out my mom's chair for her. I mean, who was he showing off for?"

Zandra shrugged. "Maybe they just teach better manners in China than they do here," she said. "My parents would love it if R.J. and Marcus acted like that."

"Well yeah, my parents loved it, too. But to me it was just so . . ."

Anna Mei's voice trailed off. She didn't seem to be able to put into words what had been so irritating about Kai Chen. Maybe it was the surprise of the whole thing. She'd expected to meet a shy, awkward boy and instead felt bulldozed by a pushy, know-it-all one. Encouraged by his parents, he dominated the conversation at dinner, talking about all the different countries he'd lived in and all the people he had met, including someone who was apparently a very famous

Chinese artist, although Anna Mei had certainly never heard of him.

Meanwhile, she spent the whole time giving one-word answers and pretending it wasn't weird having an obnoxious, world-traveling kid from China sitting next to her at dinner.

But never mind. Zandra was obviously bored with the whole topic and anxious to get going. Like a coiled up ball of energy, Zandra always preferred to be in motion. It didn't matter now anyway. Anna Mei had been as polite to the Chens as she could, and since Kai wouldn't need her as his personal welcoming committee after all, she wouldn't have to spend any more time with him.

"Forget it," she said to Zandra, shoving her apple into her pocket to eat later. "Let's go."

Chapter Eight

The Last Person

On Thursday morning, Anna Mei was surprised to find her mother sitting in the kitchen, sipping coffee and reading the paper. Her blond hair was held back with a headband, and her pullover sweater matched her blue eyes exactly. Anna Mei's father had once called Mom his "tall, beautiful Danish flower." She remembered feeling a little sad to know that *she* would never be compared to a tall, Danish anything. Physical resemblance was something she and her mother would never share.

"Good morning," Mom said, smiling over her coffee mug. "I poured your cereal and juice. How would you like a ride to school today?"

"Sure," Anna Mei said, sitting down at the table and reaching for the milk. The day was off to a good start—her breakfast was ready and she wouldn't have to ride the bus. "But why are you up already?"

Usually when her mother worked until midnight, she slept in the next morning, and Anna Mei didn't see her until after school.

"Your father went in to work early and I couldn't get back to sleep. I decided I might as well get up and get some errands done. Yogurt?"

Anna Mei shook her head. "No, thanks. I thought Dad was supposed to work *less* now that Dr. Chen is here, not more."

"In theory, that's what's supposed to happen," Mom said. "But Dr. Chen keeps getting to the lab by seven. So your dad felt he should do the same, at least for a while."

"Great," Anna Mei said, taking her empty bowl to the sink. "It's a whole family of over-achievers."

"Now why would you say that?" Mom asked.

Anna Mei paused. She had planned to share her opinion that Kai seemed like someone who would set his alarm for five o'clock every morning, just to read the encyclopedia for a few hours before breakfast.

But even as the words formed in her head, she realized they didn't sound very nice. Besides, there was no point in spending any more time thinking about him, nicely or not.

"Nothing," she said. "I'm glad Dad's getting some help with his project. Do you think he'll be able to come to my game tonight?"

"The first game of the tournament? He wouldn't miss it for the world," Mom said.

The carpool lane moved quickly, so Anna Mei ended up with plenty of time to get to class before the bell rang. There was always a short homeroom period first, where the teacher took attendance and the school office made announcements. Then everyone stayed in that room for their first class, which for Anna Mei was English.

At least, it *used* to be English, but for some reason they called it *language arts* in junior high. Danny once joked that English class must have gotten a promotion, and that if all the classes worked very hard, they could get promoted someday, too. Then science would become *experimental arts*, history would be known as *transcending time arts*, and math would upgrade to *numerical information systems*.

She was thinking of that and smiling to herself as she walked down the hall with Maddie Armstrong, her locker neighbor.

"Ready for the test today?" Maddie asked.

"Yeah, prepositions aren't too bad," Anna Mei said. "In other words, I think it's a subject in which I can do well."

Maddie grinned. "Good, then you're someone around whom I would like to be."

They were both laughing as they reached the door,

but Anna Mei's laughter died in her throat at the sight that met her there. As usual, seventh graders filled the room, chatting as they slipped into their seats, pulling notebooks and pencils from their backpacks. Mrs. Atkins was standing in her usual spot near her desk.

Only instead of greeting everyone as she normally did, Mrs. Atkins was deep in conversation with just one person—the last person Anna Mei ever expected to see there.

Chapter Nine

Some Kind of Mistake

For a moment Anna Mei couldn't move. Her feet seemed rooted to the spot where she stood, just inside the classroom door. Her brain didn't seem to be working right either. She couldn't come up with a single answer to the question that was ricocheting around inside it—*what was Kai Hao Chen doing here?*

"Oh, here's Anna Mei now," Mrs. Atkins said, smiling as if this was just an ordinary Thursday at Westside Junior High, instead of an episode from some crazy sci-fi show. Slowly, almost without her permission, Anna Mei's feet started to move, crossing what seemed like a mile and a half of tiled floor between her and the two of them.

"Kai was just telling me that you two already

know each other," Mrs. Atkins said. "And it appears you have several classes together."

Classes together? It didn't make sense. He was only eleven—he was supposed to be in sixth grade. Besides, the Chens' hotel was near the university, in a city fifteen miles away. Why wasn't Kai *there*, meeting *those* teachers?

"I'm . . . surprised to see you here," she managed to say. "I thought—"

The bell rang then, cutting off the rest of her sentence.

"Go ahead and take your seat, Anna Mei," Mrs. Atkins said. Then, in a louder voice, "All right, class, it's time for morning announcements. Let's have some quiet, please."

A loudspeaker mounted over the door came to life with a long beep, followed by a greeting from Mrs. Langley, the school secretary. Anna Mei heard something about a bus that was running late, a soccer practice that had been canceled, and a last-minute change in the lunch menu. But who could possibly be interested in any of that at a time like this?

Finally Mrs. Langley wished everyone a good day and signed off.

"Class, I have my own announcement today," Mrs. Atkins said. "This is Kai Chen, who comes to us from Beijing, China. His father is a professor on assignment at the university, so Kai will be joining our homeroom for the next few months."

Listening to her talk gave Anna Mei a weird sensation of reliving something that had happened before.

"Our new student . . . just moved here from Boston . . . do your best to make her feel welcome . . ."

But the voice in her head wasn't Mrs. Atkins—it was Ms. Wagner, her homeroom teacher at Elmwood last year. For a moment Anna Mei was back in Room 117, on the first day of sixth grade in her new school. Even now she felt her cheeks grow hot at the memory of standing there, afraid and shy, while twenty-three kids she didn't know all stared at the new girl.

"Anna Mei, since you two are already friends, I'll count on you to help Kai find his way around for the next few days. All right?"

Anna Mei blinked, trying to get her brain to focus on what was happening right now. Not only was Mrs. Atkins waiting for an answer, but now everyone in the whole class was looking at her instead of Kai.

"But we're not really . . . I mean, we just . . ." *Ugh*. Here she was stammering all over the place as if *she* was the new kid. "Yes, Mrs. Atkins," she finally managed to say.

Mrs. Atkins directed Kai to an empty desk in the second row. It was hard to concentrate with him there, especially since he didn't exactly try to keep a low profile. He kept raising his hand when Mrs. Atkins asked questions. And when she handed out the test on prepositional phrases, he got right to work on it, even though he hadn't studied for it in advance. He was one of the first to finish, too.

When the bell rang, Kai showed Anna Mei the class schedule he'd been given. They both had American history next, followed by computer lab. Because it was Thursday, she had her Spanish elective during fourth period, but his schedule didn't list an elective. She figured that meant he had lunch then, but after computer lab he decided to go back to the office to check.

Watching him go, Anna Mei wondered for the billionth time if this was really happening. A few days ago she hadn't even met Kai Chen, and now he was like her little shadow—okay, her slightly *bigger* shadow. It was all so annoying.

When the bell rang after Spanish class, she practically broke the all-time speed record getting to her locker. She couldn't wait to see her friends so she could tell them what a weird morning she'd had. Being with them would make everything seem normal again.

"Wow, Anna Mei, what are you so hyper about?" Zandra asked, pulling her lunch bag out of her locker while Anna Mei waited, apparently not so patiently. "Does this have anything to do with Kai Chen showing up here today?"

"How did you know about that?" Anna Mei asked, surprised. She and Zandra didn't have any classes together in the mornings.

"Are you kidding? *Everyone* knows about it. Did you think people wouldn't notice you walking down the hall with him?"

Anna Mei groaned. *Great.* Now the whole school was going to think they were friends—or worse, that he was her *boyfriend.*

"I can't believe this," she said, as they walked toward the cafeteria. "I mean, what's he even *doing* here?"

"Didn't you ask him?"

"I've barely even talked to him," Anna Mei said. "Basically he just followed me from class to class. But it must be some kind of mistake. They must have—"

Suddenly Zandra grabbed her arm. They'd reached the door of the cafeteria, but Zandra pulled her back into the hallway, letting other seventh graders stream past them on their way to lunch.

"What?" Anna Mei asked, confused. "Is something wrong?"

"I hate to tell you this," Zandra said, "but I think that 'mistake' is sitting at our table—right next to Danny and Luis."

Chapter Ten

An Accelerated Student

For a split second Anna Mei considered bailing out. She pictured herself walking down the hall to the office, where she would call her mother to come and pick her up. Then she would go straight up to her room, pull Cleo into her lap, and pretend this day never happened.

But in the next second, she pushed the thought away. For one thing, experience had taught her something about running away. And that "something" was that it just didn't work. Ignoring problems never made them go away—it just made them more powerful, more threatening. In the end it was always better to face things head on and figure out a way to deal with them.

Besides, she'd fought a hard-won battle since she

moved here. It hadn't been easy leaving her old house and school and friends behind—her old *life*, really. But after a rocky start she had made new friends, gotten used to a new life. Nothing—or should she say no one?—was going to make her turn and run now.

"Fine, whatever," she said to Zandra. "Obviously Kai needs to hang around with me because he doesn't know anyone else yet. After a few days I'm sure he'll move on."

Zandra gave her arm a little squeeze before letting go. "That's the spirit," she said, like the supportive teammate she was, on and off the court.

"So let's get this over with," Anna Mei said. Pinning what she hoped was a bright smile on her face, she walked into the cafeteria and straight to the table where the three boys sat.

"Hi!" she said, slipping into her usual spot, across from Danny. "I was going to introduce you guys, but I see you've already met."

Kai, sitting on Danny's right, glanced up from the tray of cafeteria food in front of him. It looked like he hadn't touched it yet. "Mrs. Langley introduced us," he said.

"Really?" she asked. "How did that happen?"

"Mrs. Atkins sent me to the office to get a projector," Danny explained. "And there was Kai, talking to Mrs. Langley about his schedule. When I found out he had fifth period lunch, I told him he should come and sit with us."

Anna Mei had to fight the urge to glare at him. She usually appreciated Danny's charm and outgoing personality, but couldn't he have dialed it down a little, just once?

"Great," she answered, still smiling. At this rate her cheek muscles would be sore by sixth period. "That's really . . . great."

Zandra had pulled a chair over and now sat directly across from Kai. "Hi," she said. "Welcome to Westside. I'm Zandra."

"Otherwise known as Miss School Spirit," Danny added, grinning at her.

"Well, I do think it's a pretty nice school," she admitted, "even though it's probably not as exciting as some of the other places Kai's been."

"Um, hello?" That was Luis, sitting on Kai's left. "He's just been telling Danny and me about his last school—the one in London. London, *England.* I'd say 'not quite as exciting' is pretty much an understatement."

Kai was looking closely at a piece of ravioli he had speared with his fork. "London was fine," he said. "I liked Barcelona better, but I would say Sydney was the most interesting."

Anna Mei had heard all about the Chens' world travels at dinner last Sunday. She wasn't about to let lunch turn into a travelogue, too. Besides, she had questions, and she was determined to get some answers.

"But aren't you a little young for junior high?" she asked, before anyone could ask what was so great about Barcelona. "I mean, you're only eleven, right?"

He set his fork down with the ravioli still on it. "I turned eleven in May," he said. "But the schools here are behind others I have attended. My placement tests indicated the seventh grade level for most subjects, higher for math and science."

"Wow," Zandra said. "That's impressive."

Danny gave a low whistle. "Not too shabby," he said. "Looks like you'll be getting some competition around here, Anna Mei."

Kai seemed intrigued by this. "So you are an accelerated student, too?"

She could have shaken Danny. Why was he dragging her into this? The last person she wanted to be compared with was Kai Chen.

Luckily Luis saved her from having to answer. "Don't pay any attention to Danny," he told Kai, with a good-natured grin. "He thinks anyone who likes school and actually does all the homework must be a genius."

"Oh. That is very . . . interesting."

Meaning, Anna Mei thought, *that it's the least interesting thing he's ever heard.*

Now Kai was examining one of his pear slices, sniffing it before taking a tentative bite.

"Is something wrong with your lunch?" Danny asked, having already devoured every last bite of his.

Kai wrinkled up his nose in the universal language that meant *this smells bad*. "It is not . . . very appetizing," he said.

Luis laughed. "That sounds like a polite way of saying that cafeteria food stinks. It's okay, Kai, *most* of us already knew that." He shot a meaningful look at Danny's empty plate.

"Hey, it's all good," Danny said with a shrug. "In fact, I think I'll go and get another carton of milk. Anybody else want one?"

After he'd gone, Zandra and Luis decided to go outside and get some fresh air before the bell rang. It was just the opportunity Anna Mei needed.

"I still don't understand how you ended up at Westside, Kai," she said. "It's a pretty long way from where your family lives."

All this time he'd been sitting there calmly, picking at his food. But now when he looked at her, his dark eyes flashed with what looked like anger. "Perhaps you should you ask your father that," he said.

Chapter Eleven

Small Town America

At first she thought she heard him wrong. Her father had met Kai Chen exactly once—how could he possibly have anything to do with this?

But before she could even get the question out, he was already answering it.

"My father said we would rent a house near the university," he said, scowling at her. "That is what we always do when we leave Beijing for my father's work. That is where you find the best schools, the most interesting people. But then your father told him how much *your* family likes it *here*."

On the word "here" Kai looked around the cafeteria, wrinkling his nose the same way he had done when sniffing the ravioli. Only this time it was as if the whole room smelled sour to him. Or maybe it was the people in it. Maybe to him, Westside's seventh graders were just a bunch of backward kids who had probably never traveled anywhere more exotic than Canada.

"Now my father believes this will be an interesting experience for me, living in what he calls 'small town America.'"

Somehow he made that familiar little phrase sound ridiculous.

Anna Mei's mouth felt dry, as if listening to Kai spit out his true feelings had made her ability to speak disappear. She had to force her words out.

"Well . . . maybe it will," she said. "Maybe you'll even end up liking it here."

He looked at her again, his eyes narrowing. "The house we have just rented does not have wireless internet service," he said, as if this explained how absurd her suggestion was. "People here use *dial-up*."

Then without waiting for a response, he pulled his neatly-folded schedule out of his pocket and laid it on the table. "This says my next class is algebra, room one hundred twenty, with Mr. Del—Mr. Del . . . ." He struggled with the name.

"Delvecchio," she told him. "That's in the eighth grade hallway, near the library."

"Thank you. I am sure I will find it."

She watched him place his tray of uneaten food in the tub near the kitchen, the way he had seen other kids do, then head for the cafeteria door. Danny, on his way back to their table, called out, "See you around, Kai!"

Sitting next to Anna Mei as she finally started gulping down her own lunch, Danny asked, "So does this mean you're off duty for now?"

"I hope it means I'm off duty forever," she said, between bites.

"Really?" Danny asked, looking puzzled. "He seems like a nice kid to me."

"Huh. You wouldn't say that if you'd been here five minutes ago."

She sounded as grouchy as she felt. Naturally, Kai had waited until all her friends were gone before letting his true personality show. It ticked her off. She'd just been minding her own business, trying to have a normal day at school, enjoying lunch with her friends, and getting ready for the game tonight—

The game tonight! The thought hit her just as the bell rang to signal the end of lunch. Her volleyball tournament started in a few hours. *I can't waste any more time and energy thinking about Kai and his crazy ideas.*

"Never mind," she said, gulping down her juice. "We need to get going."

They both had science class next, and Miss Haynes wasn't exactly shy with the tardy slips.

Hours later, feeling exhausted, Anna Mei flopped

into bed. She was sure she would fall asleep instantly. Instead she lay awake for a long time, watching the day's events parade through her head over and over again, like a TV show she couldn't turn off.

It always started at the moment she walked into English class. She felt again the shock of seeing Kai Chen there, at such an unexpected place and time. She saw herself walking through the halls with him while everyone stared. And she saw the look on his face when he told her what a huge disappointment Westside was, and how her father was to blame.

After lunch she had tried to push the whole upsetting morning out of her mind. But then Kai showed up in her social studies class, where Mr. Crandall directed him to a seat near hers. Every time he called attention to himself by raising his hand, she squirmed a little lower in her seat.

Worst of all, she relived the volleyball game, where she let her teammates down by foot faulting on her serve and getting distracted by the ball when she should have been watching the hitter. Luckily, the others had been able to compensate for her mistakes and won the game anyway. On the bus ride back to school, everyone told her to forget about it—they knew she would do better next time. But she still found it hard to join in their happy chatter and victory chants.

Her parents, who had come to the game, met the bus at school. They offered to take her out for a celebratory ice cream sundae, but Anna Mei told them she was too tired and would rather go another time. On the drive home, her father wanted to talk about the Chens.

"Jin just told me about their change of plans this morning," he said. "He seemed very enthusiastic about Kai going to Westside. Did he end up in any of your classes?"

"English, history, computers and social studies," she said, managing to restrain herself from pointing out what a ridiculously long list that was. "And he ate lunch with us. Apparently he qualified for eighth grade math and science, though."

"That's really great," Dad said, smiling broadly. "I know Kai will appreciate your being there to help him out."

It was a weird situation, she realized. Part of her wanted to tell her father what Kai had said at lunch. But in a strange role-reversal way, she felt protective of him. Hearing about her conversation with Kai would hurt Dad's feelings, and she didn't want to be the one to do that, even if she was only the messenger.

"He seems to really enjoy school," she said, sidestepping the issue of whether it was "great" having Kai there. "I'm sure he'll do just fine."

Now she rolled over in bed for what seemed to be the millionth time, trying to work it all out. No matter how much he annoyed her, she couldn't ignore the fact that Kai Chen was the new kid, and she certainly remembered how *that* felt. Besides, if she were being honest, she'd have to admit that she'd been pretty angry about moving here, too, at first.

And I did promise Dad, she thought. *I want him to know he can count on me, no matter what.*

It was the last thing she remembered thinking before finally falling asleep.

Chapter Twelve

Absolutely Bonzer

After their shaky start on Thursday, the Westside Junior High Girls' Volleyball Team came roaring back on Saturday to beat two more teams and win the district title. The final match was especially hard-fought, as the teams passed the lead back and forth. Then Zandra leaped up to spike the ball in the final rally, giving Westside the win by two points.

On the bus ride home, Zandra couldn't stop smiling. "I'm so pumped!" she said. "Wouldn't it be amazing to win regionals, too?"

Anna Mei had to grin at her friend's boundless enthusiasm. "My grandmother used to call that 'counting your chickens.' Maybe we should just concentrate on winning the next game for now."

"You sound just like Coach," Zandra said. "But a girl can dream, can't she?"

On Monday morning, Anna Mei went to school in an optimistic mood. Not only was she excited about her team's victory, she felt good about her decision to keep her promise to Dad. From now on, when it came to Kai, she would do her best to be friendly and helpful.

It didn't take long to figure out the flaw in that plan. In the very first class of the day, Mrs. Atkins called on Kai during a discussion about slang and idioms.

"These can vary widely, even among countries that speak the same language," she said. "Have you experienced this, Kai?"

"Yes, Mrs. Atkins," he said. "In America you speak English, but it is not always the same English I heard in England or Australia."

"Can you give us some examples?" she prompted.

"When I lived in London," he told her, "people said *brill* when they meant good."

"That's funny," one of the girls said. "What if something was bad?"

"Then it was *naff*. Something that you call silly or ridiculous, they would call *a load of codswallop*."

As the room erupted in laughter, he went on to explain how people in London said *chuffed* instead of happy, *scrummy* instead of delicious. If things were going well, some people said they were *tickety-boo*, but if you made a mistake, you *dropped a clanger*. In

Sydney, he said, friends were called *cobbers*, while people in your family were your *rellies*.

"If something was truly great, people there called it *absolutely bonzer*."

It took a while for Mrs. Atkins to get everyone settled down after that. But instead of being upset by the disruption, she smiled at Kai and thanked him for enlightening the class with his "specialized knowledge."

That afternoon, Anna Mei heard a couple of boys call out a greeting to Kai in the hallway, saying he was absolutely bonzer for making English class so much fun. "Usually it's a bunch of codswallop," they said, cracking themselves up.

On Tuesday, Anna Mei arrived at lunch a few minutes late and found Danny, Zandra, and Luis deep in conversation with Kai about the Barcelona soccer team.

"In Barcelona, everyone watches *fútbol*," he was explaining, using the Spanish word for the sport. "Even the smallest children know the names of all the players on the national team."

"Did you get to see any games?" Zandra asked, her voice eager.

"Of course," Kai answered. "We went as guests of the university. My father had a very important position there. Attending *fútbol* games with colleagues was expected."

"*Fantástico*," Luis exclaimed, his dark eyes

shining. "I'd give anything to see Messi and Suárez play in person!"

On Wednesday, in social studies class, Mr. Crandall announced that they would be starting the section on Asian culture soon. He pulled down a screen with a giant world map on it, then pointed to the largest continent.

"Excluding Russia, the largest country in that region is China," he said. "We're fortunate to have two Chinese natives in our class, who I'm sure will bring a unique and valuable perspective to our study. Anna Mei, exactly which part of China are you from?"

She looked up, startled. No one had ever asked her that before. "I was born in the Hunan province," she answered, "but I don't know much about it. I mean, I'll have to learn about it just like everyone else."

"I see," he said. She wondered if she was imagining a note of disappointment in his voice, as if he was feeling the whole "unique and valuable perspective" thing slipping out of his grasp. "And what about you, Kai?"

"My birthplace is Beijing," Kai said. "I have also visited many other parts of China. When I was a very small child, my parents took me to the Great Wall, to stand on the steps built by my ancestors."

"Fascinating," Mr. Crandall said, smiling now as he tugged on the screen to rewind it. "I'll look forward to hearing much more about it."

Well, at least he has one *"unique and valuable" student in the class*, Anna Mei thought. *And we all know it isn't me.*

"For now," Mr. Crandall continued, "let's start our review of the African culture section by opening your books to page ninety-three."

With everyone around her busily turning pages, Anna Mei risked a glance at Kai. He was too busy concentrating on his book to notice.

Okay, she thought, *I get it. Kai Chen is clearly the shining star of Westside Junior High. He obviously doesn't need help fitting in.*

On the bright side, she was already pretty busy as it was. She didn't need one more thing on her to-do list. And if her father ever asked her about Kai again, she could honestly say he was doing just fine.

Chapter Thirteen

Seems Like a No-Brainer

As it turned out, Anna Mei ended up crossing one thing off her list later that day. After winning the first match of the regional game, her volleyball team lost the next two. That meant the end of both the tournament and the season.

Although it was disappointing, Anna Mei had to admit that part of her was relieved. Some of her grades had started to slip lately, and she needed to concentrate on homework for a while. Spanish class was a particular thorn in her side. When she chose it as her first semester elective, she had expected to do well. And at first she had—memorizing vocabulary words seemed to come pretty easily. But once Mr. Garza started expecting students to use all that vocabulary in actual sentences, she couldn't seem to get the hang of it. Now she had less than two months to bring up her grade before the final exam.

"Let's do something fun this weekend, to cheer ourselves up," Zandra said at lunch on Wednesday. Although basketball season would be starting soon, Zandra would have loved to bring home that volleyball trophy first. "Why don't you come over on Friday and spend the night?"

"Perfect," Anna Mei said. "A movie and popcorn night is just what we need."

"Great minds think alike," Danny said, when Anna Mei mentioned her plans to him. "I was thinking we could all go to a movie on Saturday." He named the latest installment of the *Wanderer* fantasy series, about a boy who accidently time travels and then faces all kinds of challenges on his quest to get home. "Luis and I could meet you at the theater."

By the time Anna Mei got to social studies class at the end of the day, things were definitely looking up. She managed to walk past Kai without gritting her teeth or feeling her stomach tense up.

So what if everyone else thinks he's so fascinating? she thought. *Let him be the center of attention, if that's what he wants. It doesn't make any difference to me. It doesn't change anything.*

In a few months, Kai would be gone, and she would still be here with her friends. That's all that really mattered. Besides, today was Wednesday, and that meant she had Science Club after school—the highlight of her week.

At first she had been disappointed that this year's Science Quest didn't include an astronomy option—that would have been her first choice. But when she looked at the list of project ideas Miss Haynes handed out, she was immediately drawn to the earth science section. It had been fun to see how excited her dad was when she outlined her idea to him. The basic concept had to do with biofuels—the fuels that come from plants.

She had written her proposal in her project notebook.

> Since plants are a renewable resource, it seems like a no-brainer to use biofuels instead of fossil fuels (like petroleum) to run our cars and heat our homes. But it's really not that simple. Important questions need to be answered first:
>
> 1. How much useable energy do plants produce? Will it take more energy to grow them and harvest their oils than we will get in return?
> 2. How will planting crops to use for biofuels affect the environment? Is it a good idea to cut down forests (which absorb harmful carbon dioxide) or plow up farmland (which produces food) to grow plants for fuel?
> 3. If we do use plant oil for fuel, what kind of plants will give us the best results?

For my project, I will try to answer the third
   question by testing different plants to see
   if the type of plant affects:

A.) how long it takes to grow
B.) the amount of energy it can produce.

After getting the okay from Miss Haynes, she had started by planting five identical pots with different kinds of plants: wheat, barley, corn, alfalfa, and clover. Anna Mei lined the pots up on a table in the back of the room and rigged an adjustable fluorescent lamp to a shelf above.

In the weeks since then, she had watered the plants equally, continually raising the lamp so it stayed exactly four inches above the tallest one. She used a notebook to record data, like when each plant sprouted and how much it grew—that is, increased its mass—between measurements. In a few more weeks, she would pull them up by their roots and weigh them. The final steps would be to dry the plants and weigh them again. The difference between the wet weight and the dry weight would be the biomass for each type of plant. And biomass was another word for a plant's fuel potential.

Today, as Anna Mei got out her notebook and ruler to take measurements, Miss Haynes came up behind her. "Your plants are really coming along," she said. "I'm looking forward to seeing your results."

"So am I," Anna Mei said. "And I've started studying for the earth science test, too."

In addition to presenting the results of their own experiments, Science Quest participants had to be prepared to answer all kinds of questions about their subject areas. Judges awarded points based on the team's overall knowledge, so having team members you could count on was really important. Anyone who couldn't pass the test first wouldn't be allowed to compete.

"Excellent," Miss Haynes said, nodding her approval. "It would be a shame if someone who loves science as much as you do didn't make the team. I would expect that you—"

She paused as something caught her attention at the front of the room.

"Please excuse me," she said. "It looks like our new club member has arrived."

Anna Mei was busy taking measurements, so it took a moment for this to sink in. But when it did, she whipped her head around in time to see her teacher greeting the new student with a warm smile.

Chapter Fourteen

A Reasonable Conclusion

"Hello, Kai, welcome to Science Club!" Miss Haynes said, her voice as enthusiastic as her smile. "I'm delighted you've decided to join us. Come in and meet everyone."

As Miss Haynes led Kai around the room, introducing him to the other club members and talking about their projects, it occurred to Anna Mei that she really should have seen this coming. After all, Kai was an advanced science student, taking a class meant for kids two years older than he was. And his father was a researcher, just like hers. *Of course* he would want to be in the Science Club.

She wrote some measurements down in her notebook, then realized she'd put them in the wrong column.

And whatever his project is, I'm sure it will be the best, she thought, flipping the pencil over to erase her mistake. *Not just the best one here, but the best project anywhere.* She pressed down harder on the eraser. *Ever.*

A ragged hole appeared in the paper just as Kai and Miss Haynes reached her table, and Anna Mei quickly turned her notebook over to hide it.

"Kai tells me that your fathers are working together at the university," Miss Haynes said.

"It's a project for The Great Lakes Bioenergy Research Center," Anna Mei explained.

A bright smile lit the teacher's face. "How exciting! I've thought about going into research myself one day."

"My father finds it very rewarding," Kai said.

Anna Mei turned her head just in time to hide a smirk. Somehow Kai always sounded like he was auditioning for the role of teacher's pet. While Miss Haynes went off to get a club permission slip for his parents to sign, Anna Mei went back to measuring her plants. But she was conscious of him still standing right behind her.

Why doesn't he go and hang over someone else's shoulder? she wondered. *No matter what all the teachers seem to think, we aren't actually friends. He knows that as well as I do.*

Finally Kai spoke up. "Your project is about biomass?"

She tried to keep the annoyance out of her voice as she adjusted the grow light. "Is that what Miss Haynes told you?"

"No," he said. "Your topic is earth science. You are measuring plant growth. That you are studying biomass is a reasonable conclusion."

A reasonable conclusion. She'd like to share what she had concluded about *him*. Instead she took a breath and reminded herself that it didn't matter what Kai thought or said. That thought made her turn around and face him.

"And what project are *you* going to do, Kai?" she asked, leaving out the part about how superior it was sure to be.

He shrugged. "There are many topics to choose from in the study of plants."

Great. If he did a project on the earth science list, he would be on her team for the Science Quest.

"Well, there are other choices, you know," she pointed out, trying to sound casual, as if she didn't care either way. "There's physical science, chemistry, engineering . . . you can choose any team you want."

For a moment, she thought she saw something flicker across his face, an expression of . . . what? Uncertainty? Regret? She wasn't sure, and before she could even wonder what it could mean, the look was gone.

"What *I* want," he said slowly, "is not important."

Honestly, the word "exasperating" was invented for her conversations with Kai. No matter what they talked about, she always ended up trying to figure out what he *really* meant. Then it dawned on her that maybe Miss Haynes had already assigned him to the earth science team, without discussing it with him first.

"I'm sure if you talked to Miss Haynes," she said, still trying to sound indifferent, "she wouldn't care which team you picked."

He frowned at her in a way that was becoming all too familiar, as if she had once again come up with the most ridiculous response imaginable. But what else could he mean by saying that what he wanted didn't matter?

Miss Haynes reappeared, permission slip in hand. As the two of them started talking about project ideas, Anna Mei slipped away and took a seat in the back of the room, where she could study for the earth science exam in peace.

Chapter Fifteen

Downhill in a Hurry

The next night, Anna Mei was just starting to set the table for dinner when her father came in from the garage.

"It's really getting cold out there," he said, pulling off his driving gloves. "I guess the nice fall weather is officially over."

"Well, it *is* only a week until Thanksgiving," Mom reminded him. She bent down to peer through the window on the oven door.

Dad sniffed the air. "Is that the power of suggestion," he asked, "or does it already smell like Thanksgiving around here?"

"It's stuffing," Anna Mei told him. "Mom made it for dinner."

"Wow!" Dad said. "Is this what you'd call a sneak preview?"

70

Mom smiled. "Kind of," she said, taking a potholder from its hook. "I wanted to try out a recipe I saw on a cooking show, before I serve it next week. It's made with brown bread and apples."

"Feel free to use me as your guinea pig anytime," Dad told her, stopping to kiss her cheek before heading off to hang up his coat.

Sitting around the table a few minutes later, they all agreed that the stuffing was delicious and should definitely make the cut.

"Are we having Thanksgiving at Aunt Karen's again?" Anna Mei asked, passing a bowl of green beans to her mother.

"I'm not sure," Mom said. "I'd like to take a turn hosting this year, but I'll have to work on Wednesday, so I won't get home until after midnight. You know, sometimes I wish . . ."

Her voice trailed off. Anna Mei wondered if she was going to say something about missing Boston, and the Thanksgivings they used to have there. Her mother could get pretty sentimental about holidays.

"Wish what?" Dad prompted, helping himself to more stuffing.

"It's just something I've been thinking about lately," Mom said. "It bothers me sometimes how much I'm away from home, especially at dinnertime, when you're both here."

"But you love your job at the hospital," Anna Mei

said. "You're always saying how much you like taking care of people."

Her mother smiled in that wistful way she sometimes had. "Now you see my problem," she said. "Apparently there needs to be two of me, so I can take care of everyone at the same time."

Dad reached over and covered her hand with his. "Not that we wouldn't enjoy having two of you around," he said, "but don't worry. We understand how much your patients need you. And if you want to have Thanksgiving here, you can count on us for help."

"Thanks," Mom said, squeezing his hand in return. "You two are the best."

"Exactly," Dad agreed, catching Anna Mei's eye and winking. "I'm a world class potato peeler, if I do say so myself, and Anna Mei has perfected the art of table-setting. I think she could be trusted with the good china."

It would be their first Thanksgiving in this house. Anna Mei could picture it now—the whole family sitting around the big dining room table with Grandmother Anna's delicate blue and white china spread in front of them. The scene was warm and cozy, with everyone smiling as they passed the serving platters around. The food would look and taste delicious, and afterward everyone would help with the dishes. They'd play games until it was time for Aunt Karen and Uncle Jeff to bundle up the kids and take them home. Then Dad would make popcorn while Mom got out one of those sappy old movies she liked so much.

The vision was so real she could almost taste the turkey now. "Sure, Mom," she said. "We can do it— it'll be fun."

"I'll talk to Karen and let you know what we decide," Mom said. "Oh, Greg, I almost forgot to tell you—I did speak with Lian Chen today. We've made plans to go shopping this Saturday afternoon."

"That's great," Dad said. "Jin tells me she doesn't feel comfortable going out by herself, so she spends a lot of time alone in the house. I'm sure she'll really enjoy the company."

Neither of them seemed to notice Anna Mei practically choking on her sip of milk. One minute they'd been having a normal conversation and the next minute her parents were talking about "Lian" and "Jin" as if they were good friends, instead of people they barely knew.

"You're welcome to join us, Anna Mei," Mom said. "I'm thinking of taking her to Grand Rapids, to some of the larger department stores. I'm afraid our little downtown here will be a major let-down, compared to the places she's used to shopping."

Okay, now things had gone from slightly weird to just plain crazy. It was bad enough to imagine her mother and Kai's mother hanging out together for the whole afternoon. But Anna Mei tagging along?

That was not going to happen—not in this lifetime, anyway.

"I'll still be with Zandra on Saturday afternoon," she reminded her mother, thanking her lucky stars that those plans had already been approved by both sets of parents. "We're going to meet Danny and Luis at the mall for a two o'clock movie. Mrs. Caine is driving us."

It was the perfect excuse, or at least it *would* have been, if Dad had not been there to hear it.

"That sounds like fun," he said, as he got up to start clearing dishes. "I'll bet it's something Kai would like to do. Did you think of inviting him?"

This conversation was going downhill in a hurry— somehow the Chens had managed to invade her quiet evening at home with her parents. She needed to shut this down before it went any further.

"I don't think it's really up to me, Dad," she said, following him over to the sink with her dishes. "Danny did all the planning, so I'd feel funny inviting someone without talking to him first."

"I can't imagine Danny would mind having one more person along," Dad pointed out. "He strikes me as being a 'the more, the merrier' kind of guy."

Of course, *that* was pretty hard to argue with— anyone who'd ever spent five minutes with Danny would say the same thing. She needed to try a different approach.

"I kind of doubt that Kai would be interested anyway," she said. That, at least, was a point she would have no trouble defending. "It's not like he's shy around the other kids, or has a problem meeting people. Wherever he goes he's pretty much the center of attention."

Mom was busy putting leftovers into plastic containers. "That's funny," she said. "Mrs. Chen seems just the opposite—so shy that she'd rather spend most of her time alone than meet people."

"Huh," Anna Mei said. She bit back what she was actually thinking—that it would be great if Kai had taken after his mother a lot more.

"Well, just keep it in mind," Dad said, wiping his hands on a kitchen towel. "The Chens are going to be here for a while, and helping them feel at home is the right thing to do."

"Besides, Kai could always say no if he's not interested," Mom pointed out.

Great—now they were double-teaming her. It was time to pull out the homework excuse and head upstairs, which she managed to do a few minutes later without actually promising them anything.

Chapter Sixteen

The Right Thing to Do

As it turned out, the perfect Thanksgiving scene Anna Mei had imagined was as much a fantasy as the movie she saw with her friends on Saturday.

After escaping Mom's invitation to join the shopping trip, then managing to avoid Dad's suggestion that she ask Kai to the movie, Anna Mei had figured she was safely in Chen-less territory for a while. She headed off to Zandra's in a great mood on Friday, leaving the irritations of the past few weeks behind and looking forward to spending time with her friends.

On Saturday, Danny's mother picked them all up at the theater. They spent a couple of hours at the Gallaghers' playing Danny's favorite board game. He liked to make up gruesome scenarios as he accused the characters of committing dastardly crimes in the creepy old mansion. By the time Mrs. Gallagher drove Anna Mei home, her mother was just returning from her shopping trip.

"So after she got over her initial shyness," Mom said, describing her afternoon with Mrs. Chen, "she started to open up a bit. At first we talked mostly about Kai. Her face just lit up every time she said his name. She's so proud of him, Greg—she thinks he hung the moon, as my mother used to say."

Having just spent twenty-four relaxing hours without having to think or hear about Kai Chen, Anna Mei was in no mood to do it now.

He could have actually *hung the moon, plus the sun and all the stars,* she thought, *and I* still *wouldn't want to hear about it.* She excused herself and went into the kitchen to get some juice, leaving her parents to their boring conversation.

Of course, boring was far better than the bombshell that fell a few days later, when her mother answered the phone after dinner. It turned out to be Mrs. Chen, calling to accept an invitation Mom had apparently extended at some point during their shopping trip. The Chen family would be delighted to join the Andersons for Thanksgiving dinner.

"I hope you don't mind," Mom said, finding Dad in his favorite chair in the study, paging through one of his science magazines while Anna Mei used his laptop for homework. "It just seemed like the right thing to do."

While her father insisted that of course it was the right thing to do—he'd been considering the idea himself—Anna Mei felt a rush of irritation. How could they even *think* of inviting the Chens for Thanksgiving? It was supposed to be a special family time, not a time to have just anyone over for dinner. And it wasn't fair to Aunt Karen's family, either— they'd never even *met* the Chens.

She left the room quietly, too upset to confront them about it now. Besides, she knew it would be useless to try and change their minds. For some reason, they seemed determined to treat the Chens like their new best friends. She didn't know if it was because Dad worked with Dr. Chen, or Mom felt sorry for Mrs. Chen, or they considered their long-ago visit to China to be some kind of bond between them. All she knew was that Thanksgiving would be ruined, and there was nothing she could do about it.

"Oh come on, how bad could it be?" Danny asked at school on Monday, when she complained to him. "They'll eat a little turkey, watch a little football, then go home. And you'll be left with a bunch of delicious leftovers to chow down on all weekend."

Leave it to Danny to get fixated on the food. She tried to steer him back to the point.

"It doesn't matter how long they stay—it just won't be the same with them there," she said. "Kai will probably spend the whole time trying to impress everyone. And his parents are so stuffy and formal—they won't get our family jokes or anything. That means my dad and Uncle Jeff won't goof around like they usually do. And what about Emily and Benjy? They won't like having strangers around. Benjy might even be afraid of them."

The list of why this shouldn't be happening just got longer and longer. But she was the only one who seemed to care. When Thanksgiving Day arrived, so did the Chens, exactly on time and even more dressed up than before, if that was possible.

This time they brought a dish of something called *nian gao*, which Dr. Chen translated as "sticky rice cake." Anna Mei couldn't imagine why anyone would want a dessert like that when Mom's delicious pumpkin pies sat cooling on the counter.

At least offering to take the cake to the kitchen gave Anna Mei an excuse to disappear for a while. But then Mrs. Chen followed her in there, asking for an apron and insisting on helping Mom chop vegetables. Anna Mei ended up mashing the potatoes. She figured that was a much better option than having to make conversation with Kai or his father. She'd noticed the last time they were here that the kitchen was one room they never ventured into.

When the dinner was ready, complete with brown bread stuffing, Anna Mei slipped into her seat between her mother and Emily. Her father, at the head of the table, spoke for a moment about the meal shared by the colonists and native Wampanoags at Plymouth, Massachusetts, to celebrate the harvest in 1621. Then he invited everyone to join in a prayer of thanks.

Anna Mei noticed that while her whole family immediately folded their hands and bowed their heads, the Chens sat stiffly, their hands in their laps. She thought Kai looked especially uncomfortable, and wondered for a moment what it would be like to grow up in a home where prayers weren't a natural part of the day.

When everyone was quiet, her father read "A Thanksgiving Prayer" by American poet Ralph Waldo Emerson:

For each new morning with its light,
For rest and shelter of the night,
For health and food,
For love and friends,
For everything Thy goodness sends.

Anna Mei felt her eyes sting at the unfairness of it all. A year ago she'd finally accepted that their move here was permanent—this would be her home from now on. Since then she'd begun to feel happy and secure in her new life. She had worked hard, made some really good friends, and felt truly thankful for her blessings. So why did the Chens have to come along and make everything feel wrong again?

Chapter Seventeen

Thanksgiving Ordeal

As the meal dragged on, Anna Mei tried to stay in her own little bubble, letting the conversation drift and flow around her. But Emily had other ideas.

"Don't you like the potatoes, Anna Mei?" she asked, looking at the untouched pile on her cousin's plate. "They're my favorite. I like the rolls, too. But I don't like that cranberry stuff—it's too squishy. Mom said it's okay if I just have carrots. Did you know we're having pie *and* ice cream for dessert?"

"And don't forget Mrs. Chen's rice cake," Mom added, smiling.

The unending chatter, which Anna Mei usually found amusing, somehow made her feel even more uncomfortable. She just couldn't relax, knowing that the Chens were right there listening, probably judging everything and comparing it to all the fancy places and important people they'd known.

Mrs. Chen didn't say much, of course. She smiled and nodded a lot, and seemed content to let the others talk. Anna Mei noticed that instead of just passing the serving bowls to her husband and son, so they could help themselves, she put the food on their plates for them. It was no wonder that Kai seemed so full of himself—his mother treated him like the crown prince.

To kill time while she waited for the whole ordeal to be over, she started making plans in her head for the next day, hoping to salvage as much as she could of the long holiday weekend. So at first she didn't notice that her father had stopped talking about the upcoming football game and was now talking about her.

"Of course we enjoy having her home more, now that volleyball season is over," he was saying. "But I have to admit—I'm going to miss going to her games now."

"Volleyball has a long history in China," Dr. Chen said, not even acknowledging his wife as she silently refilled his glass. "When I was a boy, most athletes were men. Now many women players have also brought honor to China."

Kai looked across the table at Anna Mei. "Who are *your* favorite women players?" he asked.

At least it was a question she could understand, and a topic she knew something about. She had gotten a crash course in women's volleyball at camp this past summer. "I like Nichole Davis," she answered easily. "She's only five foot four, but she's an amazing defender. The US Olympic team couldn't have won the silver medal in 2008 without her."

After a slight pause, Kai spoke again. "Do you have any favorite *Chinese* players?"

Anna Mei felt her muscles tense. There it was again—that thing Kai did, where he asked a question and fooled you into thinking he was being polite, but really all he wanted to do was test you. Couldn't anybody else see that?

"I'm not . . . I don't know much about Chinese players, I guess."

"But you must know Lang Ping," Kai insisted.

She shook her head.

"Jenny Lang Ping?" Kai said again, as if maybe she just hadn't heard him the first time. "The 'Iron Hammer'?" When she still looked blank he went on. "She was the coach for the 2008 US team you are so proud of. They won that medal in the city of her birth—Beijing. Before that she coached the Chinese Olympic team. They also won a silver medal." His voice rose as he grew more determined to make his point. "Before that she was—"

"Kai Hao," his father said, frowning. Something

in his voice must have meant *knock it off*, since Kai immediately went silent.

"In his enthusiasm, my son sometimes becomes overly excited," Dr. Chen said. "He is very proud of China's achievements in every discipline, including athletics."

"I did not intend disrespect, Father," Kai said. Then, as if he couldn't seem to help himself from making one last comment, "I simply expected that Anna Mei would know one of China's most famous and accomplished athletes."

Even his apology seems like an accusation, Anna Mei thought, feeling more furious by the minute. *Besides, why would I follow sports in China anyway? I'm American.*

But instead of defending her, her father just smiled. "No harm done," he said smoothly. "I think it's great that Kai is so knowledgeable about Chinese history and culture. In fact, getting to know all of you has made me want to learn much more about it myself."

It sounded like Dad planned to put learning more about China on his to-do list. That was fine for him, but as far as Anna Mei was concerned, *her* list was already full.

Chapter Eighteen

The Wondrous Gift is Given

The three weeks between Thanksgiving and the start of Christmas break flew by. All that free time Anna Mei expected to have after volleyball season seemed to vanish into the cold, frosty air. In fact, she felt busier than ever—working on her biofuel project, studying for Miss Haynes' earth science test, doing research for an English paper, trying to catch up in Spanish.

Some nights she stayed up so late that she could hardly drag herself to the bus stop in the morning. She knew winter had arrived because now she sometimes waited for the bus in the snow, but that was about the only time she was ever outside. She knew Christmas was coming because at Sunday Mass, she'd seen Luis and his sister serving at the altar, helping Fr. Mark light the first candle of Advent. But mostly the days just seemed to pass in a blur of school, homework, and projects. She was starting to worry that she wouldn't get everything done before the semester ended in January.

"Earth to Cartoon Girl," Danny said one day in the cafeteria. "Come in, please."

Anna Mei looked up from the page of science notes she'd brought to study over lunch.

"What? What's wrong?" she asked.

"That's what I'm trying to find out," he told her. "I'm starting to feel like I'm on the sidelines at a race, watching you run the forty-yard dash."

"What's that supposed to mean?" she wanted to know. "I'm just trying to get a little extra studying in, that's all."

He looked down at her half-eaten sandwich. "A little extra studying? You don't even have time to eat anymore! We talked about this a few months ago, remember? About how it's okay to not always be first or best at everything? I thought you were on board with the whole concept."

"But that's not what I'm—" The look on his face stopped her, the one that said *don't even try it, Cartoon Girl.*

"Look," he said, "I know it's important to you to get good grades and everything. But I'm worried about you. I mean, what happened to that girl who was going to stop and smell the roses? Or, considering it's December in Michigan—the pine needles?"

Anna Mei let out a sigh and put her notes down. It was nice that he cared enough to worry about her. And she *had* been pushing herself pretty hard lately. *But it's only for a little while longer*, she thought, *just until I get—*

His next question interrupted her thoughts. "This doesn't have anything to do with Kai, does it? I mean, with how smart he is?"

It took every ounce of her self-control not to just get up and walk away then. She was quite aware that Kai was the center of his own universe, and of his parents' universe, and possibly even the whole seventh-grade-at-Westside-Junior-High universe.

But *her* life certainly didn't revolve around him. How could Danny even suggest it?

She counted to ten in her head, then said slowly, "You're my friend, Danny, and I don't want to argue with you, so can we please just not talk about Kai Chen? It was bad enough that his family ruined our Thanksgiving. And for your information, I'm not competing with him—I'm just trying to catch up after volleyball season. So you can stop worrying, all right?"

Whether he decided to drop it, or he stopped because the bell rang, she would never know. She was just grateful to see him stand up and pick up his lunch tray, piled with empty dishes.

"If you say so," he said. "Come on—let's go."

Their two-week break started soon after that—a welcome change from the hectic pace Anna Mei had been keeping up. Besides, she loved all the traditions her family had at Christmastime. They decorated their tree together, and she helped her father bake the Swedish coffee cakes he liked to give his friends and co-workers. She also spent some time setting out their nativity scene on the hallway table. That tradition had started when she was a little girl, fascinated by the miniature people, animals, and angels who all played a part in the story of Christ's birth. She'd been known to rearrange the figures many times in the weeks leading up to Christmas.

One thing they did change was the Mass they attended. Back in Boston, they had always gone to the evening service on Christmas Eve, the one everyone called the "family Mass." But figuring that Anna Mei was old enough to stay up late, they decided this year to go to midnight Mass at St. Joseph's.

Draped in fresh evergreen garlands and bathed in soft candlelight, the church looked especially beautiful. An oversize, hand-carved nativity scene held a place of honor in front of the altar. At first everything was hushed, but then the choir started singing, their voices joined by piano, flutes, and strings. The words and music sent a shiver through Anna Mei as she sat in the pew between her parents.

*How silently, how silently the wondrous gift is
    given!*
*So God imparts to human hearts the blessings of
    his heaven.*

She felt her heart beat faster with the wonder
of it all—the gift of peace and hope coming into the
world in the form of a tiny little baby—born, like she
was, in a place so far away.

Chapter Nineteen

A Little More to It

By the second week of Christmas break, Anna Mei was back to studying again. She was especially worried about the final Spanish exam coming up—it would be her last chance to bring her grade up for that class. A quick phone call to Luis helped ease her mind a bit—he readily agreed to meet her after school next week for a tutoring session.

She had just hung up the phone from that call when her father bounded up the stairs to her room, still wearing his coat and scarf. His glasses were all fogged up from coming out of the cold night air.

"Great news!" he announced, so excited that she wondered if his project had just been nominated for the National Medal of Science or something. But it turned out that his excitement was for his other passion—basketball.

"I scored four tickets to the Spartan game tomorrow night," he said. "It's been sold out for a while, but the guy I got them from can't go after all. And they're great seats—practically on the floor."

"Sounds like fun," Anna Mei agreed. "So if all three of us go, I can invite Zandra for the fourth ticket. Danny would have loved it, too, but he's still in Indiana at his grandparents'."

"Unfortunately, it's a night your mom is working," Dad said, unbuttoning his coat. "But I've already figured that out. I invited Dr. Chen and Kai to go with us. That way we'll each have someone to buddy up with. Great idea, right?"

For a moment she just looked at him, hoping maybe she'd dozed off while studying her Spanish vocabulary list, and this was some kind of homework-induced hallucination.

But when she blinked, he was still there, as real as the pencil in her hand and the book in her lap. And he was waiting for an answer.

Are you crazy? was the first one that came to mind, but she figured a more low-key approach might work better. "Not really," she said, a lot more calmly than she felt. "I hardly know Kai. He just happens to go to my school."

Her father's smile faded. "Well, there's a little more to it than that," he said. "We're friends with the whole Chen family. Remember, I'm trying to make them feel at home here."

"That's great, Dad," she said, sincerely. "I'm glad they have you looking out for them."

"But not just me," he insisted, now shrugging off his coat and sitting down on the bed next to Cleo. This was obviously not going the way he'd expected. "Your mom has taken Mrs. Chen under her wing, and you agreed to help out with Kai."

"Right," she said, nodding. "I agreed to show him around school, introduce him to people, and help him with homework. But everyone knows who he is now, Dad. They practically fight over who gets to sit with him at lunch. He gets As in every class without even trying. I'd say he's way past needing my help."

It seemed pretty simple to her. Hopefully he would see that, too.

"But it wasn't just about *helping* Kai. What I meant was . . . it was more like . . ." It was weird to see him struggling for words. He usually sounded so sure of himself. Finally he said, "I see how much fun you have with your friends. I thought it would be great if Kai was your friend, too."

Okay, forget the low-key approach. She'd been feeling a little bad about disappointing her father, but this was too much.

"Come on, Dad, I'm turning thirteen in a few weeks," she told him, frowning. "I think that's old enough to pick my own friends, don't you? I mean, I can't like someone just because you want me to."

"Well . . . no," he said, looking a little startled by

this answer. He took off his glasses and rubbed the spot above his nose where they sat. "I didn't mean that, Anna Mei. I guess I just . . . hoped that you *would* like him. That you would *want* to be his friend, that's all."

Anna Mei knew she should just let it go, but something about those words seemed to strike a match inside her, igniting an explosion. She heard her voice rising but couldn't stop it. "Why—because we have so much in common? I hope you don't think that, Dad, because I don't want to be anything like Kai Chen. I think he's stuck up and phony and . . . and just plain obnoxious! And he's always talking to me about how great China is, and acting like there's something wrong with me for not knowing—or caring—all about it."

Her father didn't answer at first. She understood why he'd be surprised, since she'd tried to keep her opinion of Kai pretty much to herself. But with this crazy idea about the basketball game, Dad had given her no choice—she had to set him straight.

Finally he stood up and put his glasses back on, then picked up his coat. "All right," he said, "message received. I'm still taking the Chens to the game, but I'll see if your Uncle Jeff can use your ticket."

He walked over to the door, but instead of leaving, he turned to look at her. "There's just one thing, though, that I want you to think about, okay? Kai was born to Chinese parents, which makes him

Chinese. Where he travels or where he lives doesn't change that about him."

Well, *that* little fact seemed obvious, and not something she needed him to point out.

"And where *you* live doesn't change it, either, Anna Mei." he said. "You're Chinese, too, remember?"

She was relieved when he actually left this time. It saved her from having to point out that of course she remembered she was born in China, and that ever since the Chens had arrived in town, it's all anyone seemed to talk about.

Although she knew her father was disappointed to hear how she felt, there was an upside to all this. Maybe now he would stop trying to push Kai into her plans. When his project was finished and the Chens moved away—then things would get back to the way they used to be. It couldn't happen too soon, as far as she was concerned.

Chapter Twenty

Buen Amigo

"This has been a huge help, Luis," Anna Mei said, a few days later. The two of them were sitting at a table in the cafeteria, making use of the open study hall available after school. For the past hour and a half, Luis had been patiently helping her make sense of the Spanish language. "You're a really great friend."

Luis smiled. *"En español, por favor."*

"Wow, you sound just like Mr. Garza," Anna Mei told him. "You should consider a career in teaching. Okay, I'll give it a try: *Gracias. Tú eres un . . . amigo bueno."*

"Buen amigo," he corrected. "But that was very close—I think you have the hang of it now. Try not to get so stressed out and you'll do fine."

"I hope so. My plan is to take at least two years of Spanish in high school, so I'd hate to go down in flames before I even get there. And I've heard that French is even harder."

Luis unscrewed the cap on the bottle of juice Anna Mei had bought him from a vending machine as a token of her appreciation.

"I wonder if they teach Chinese at the high school," he said, taking a sip. "I know there's more than one dialect, but Kai said that Mandarin is the most common."

Ugh. What was this obsession everyone seemed to have with talking to her about Kai? First Danny, then her father, and now Luis. It even sounded like Luis was implying that if the high school offered Chinese, she would naturally want to take it.

"Why?" she asked, deciding to challenge him. "Are *you* interested in learning Mandarin?"

He shrugged. "I don't know. Maybe." Then he grinned. "There wouldn't be much point in me taking Spanish, would there?"

"I guess not," she agreed.

That made her think of something she hadn't really considered before. Luis looked as Mexican as she did Chinese. Maybe more than anyone else, he would understand how annoying it was to have people make assumptions based on that.

"Luis," she said, realizing she wasn't sure how to start. "I'm wondering if . . . well, if it ever bothers you that because you look a certain way, people think . . . certain things about you?"

"You mean because I'm so tall, dark, and handsome?" he asked, that familiar twinkle in his eyes. His sense of humor wasn't as goofy as Danny's, but he could always be counted on to come up with a witty line.

"Besides that," she said, grinning at his joke before trying again. The last thing she wanted to do was offend him. "What I mean is, you were born and raised right here in Michigan, just like most of the kids in this room." She waved her arm in the direction of the other tables, many of them occupied by seventh and eighth graders getting in their own extra studying. "But because you look Mexican, people expect you to speak Spanish, right? And to know a lot about the country your ancestors came from?"

Luis set his juice down on the table and leaned back in his chair. He hesitated, as if he'd realized that her question was a serious one, and he wanted to give her a thoughtful answer. Finally he said, "I see what you're getting at, but I'm not sure I'm the right person to ask. The thing is, I do speak Spanish, and I do know a lot about Mexico—I've even been there. Whether people expect that or not doesn't really come into it. It's just who I am."

"I guess our situations really aren't the same," she said. "What I mean is, you're more Mexican than I am

Chinese. I didn't grow up learning all that stuff, like you did."

"Well, not everyone does," he pointed out. "But my parents and grandparents always tell us kids that we're Mexican *and* American. They think it's important for us to honor both parts of our heritage. So we keep some of the traditions from Mexico, like celebrating *Las Posadas* at Christmas time, and making special foods like *pan dulce*. But we also have turkey on Thanksgiving, and watch fireworks on the Fourth of July. It seems like I get to have the best of both worlds."

When she didn't answer right away he leaned forward again. "Has someone been giving you a hard time, Anna Mei?" he asked.

"Not exactly," she said, with a sigh. "It's just that . . . ever since Kai got here, I've heard the word 'Chinese' more than I ever did in my whole life. And I've just never thought of myself that way. When we gave our heritage reports last year, I told the class everything I know about my birth mother and the orphanage, which took about two sentences. But Kai keeps expecting me to know all kinds of things about China. Even Mr. Crandall seems disappointed that I don't have anything interesting to say about it."

Luis ran a hand through his black hair, a familiar gesture that usually meant he was thinking. "I guess it's different for you," he said. "It seems like you have to make a choice that I didn't—whether to learn more about your heritage or not. I just hope whatever you decide is what *you* want, and not what other people expect."

She had to smile then. "You make that sound so easy," she told him. "As if figuring out what I want isn't the hardest part of all."

"Hey, I'm just your Spanish tutor," he said, grinning back at her. "Counseling services are extra."

"I see. As in *mucho dinero*?"

He laughed. "*Sí, mi amiga*. As they say: priceless."

"Then, we should probably get going," she said, smiling as she started to gather up her books. "I obviously can't afford to—"

"Hey, Kai!" someone called out. "Come and sit with us, okay?"

Anna Mei looked up and saw Kai heading toward a table of eighth graders. "We're having trouble with this math worksheet," one of them said, pulling out a chair for him.

No matter where he goes, she thought, *people always seem to scoot over and make room for him.*

Chapter Twenty-One

Nothing Like Him

Luis may not have had all the answers to life's questions, but his hints about conquering beginning Spanish sure did the trick. Anna Mei managed to get an A on the final test, which brought her grade for the class up to a B. Not as good as she would have liked, but at least it wasn't completely embarrassing.

With the start of the new semester, her elective switched to yearbook. She'd loved working on the Elmwood Elementary yearbook last year, so starting this class was exciting. Of course, when she'd signed up for it in the fall, Anna Mei imagined Danny sitting next to her just as he had at Elmwood. His imaginative sketches had been a highlight of that yearbook.

But with Swim Club starting, and his art elective switching to Spanish, Danny had decided he wouldn't have time to work on the yearbook. Sometimes the staff had to meet after school, and he didn't want to be away from home that much.

Anna Mei was disappointed, but she understood how he felt. Before she'd met him, Danny's mother had gone though cancer treatments. Those were some pretty rough times for the Gallagher family. Now Mrs. Gallagher was feeling much better, working at the public library and participating in a cancer support group. Danny's father had cut back on his work schedule, so he was home for dinner almost every night. Even Danny's brother Connor was spending more time with them, especially now that football season was over.

Yearbook wasn't the only positive thing about the new semester—Science Club was going well, too. With her plants all measured, dried, and weighed, Anna Mei was ready to start writing her report and constructing a display board. Better still, she'd passed the earth science test with an almost perfect score. Along with fifteen other students, she was now officially a member of the Westside Junior High School Science Quest Team.

She tried not to dwell on the fact that Kai Chen was one of the other fifteen. Because he joined the club late, he didn't have time to set up and run an experiment. Instead he was creating an elaborate display about how plants can act as "carbon sinks," absorbing some of the carbon dioxide that results from burning fossil fuels. According to Kai, people in the United Kingdom and Australia had started planting rooftop gardens and changing their farming methods in order to encourage more carbon absorption.

"I realize we don't know if you'll still be here in March for the regional competition," Miss Haynes told him when announcing the test results, "but the work you've done so far is excellent. For now we'll proceed with you on the team. One of the alternates can always step in and take your place if necessary."

Anna Mei had to admit that Kai's project was pretty interesting, and that the team would be stronger with him on it. Still, a little part of her was rooting for that "alternate" scenario. It would mean that by March, Kai and his family would have moved on to their next assignment, where he could feel free to start making someone else's life miserable.

Her plan for getting through until that happened was to just ignore him as much as possible. But then Kai had to go and join the Swim Club, so he was spending a lot more time with Danny. And that meant *she* had to hear about it.

"He's really a good swimmer," Danny said one day, as he and Anna Mei headed down the hall after the dismissal bell. "Even though he's younger than everyone else, he has a lot of speed."

Anna Mei rolled her eyes. "What a surprise," she said, "Kai Chen is good at something."

"Sarcasm noted," Danny said, stopping at his

locker. "But you know, some people might say the same thing about you."

"Then *some* people might need to get their eyes checked, so they can see that I'm nothing like him," she shot back, her voice sounding a little more shrill than she intended.

Danny stayed low-key, shrugging as he turned the dial on his lock. "Well, in my humble opinion, you're both smart and funny and good at a lot of things. I mean, think about it—if I didn't like that kind of person, I wouldn't like *you*."

"Oh, come on, Danny," she insisted. "Kai Chen is like the exact opposite of me when I was the new kid. He's confident, outgoing, popular—and he doesn't care at all about fitting in. He's too full of himself to worry about stuff like that."

"I don't know," Danny said, shoving his books in the locker and grabbing his gym bag. "I think you could be wrong about that. After all, you were pretty sure *I* was a jerk when you first met me, remember? How long did it take you to figure out what a great guy I really am?"

"Actually, I'm still waiting," she answered, making him grin as he hurried off to swimming practice.

It was easy to fall back on their familiar routine of poking fun at each other, but the truth was that his words had stung a little. Now even Danny was telling her that she was wrong about Kai. Why didn't anyone else see him the way she did?

Chapter Twenty-Two

The Year of the Tiger

"Thirteen! It's just not possible that in a few days, I'll be the father of a teenager."

It was the twenty-fifth of January, four days before Anna Mei's birthday. Dad had just come home from work to find her and her mother in the kitchen making plans.

"I know you'd like it better if I started aging backward from now on," Anna Mei teased him. "But look at the bright side—you still have a few years before I get my driver's license."

He clutched at his chest and staggered around the room in mock horror. Then he stopped to look over Anna Mei's shoulder as she did a search on the laptop. "How are the plans coming along?" he asked. "Do they include a house full of other almost-teenagers?"

"Actually, I think you're off the hook this year," Anna Mei told him. "I'm looking up times for the new show at the planetarium. My idea is to invite Zandra, Luis, and Danny out to dinner at Delaney's on Friday, then go to the show."

She held her breath for a moment, hoping no one would mention the word "Kai." The basketball game had been bad enough—what would she do if they insisted that she invite Kai to her birthday party, of all things?

"Plus we're having Karen, Jeff, and the kids over for a family celebration on Sunday," Mom added. "Cake, ice cream, presents—the works."

"Sounds good," Dad said. "Count me in for cake decorating, chauffeuring, clown duty—whatever you need to make it a birthday to remember."

Anna Mei smiled, relieved that he seemed to have put the incident with the basketball tickets behind them. "You in a clown costume *would* be memorable," she told him, "but for all the wrong reasons."

Dad slipped off his coat and went to the hallway closet. "I think I'll go up and take a shower before dinner," he said, grabbing a hanger. "I went for a run at lunchtime and didn't have—oh, I almost forgot about this."

He came back into the kitchen carrying a square white envelope he'd found in his coat pocket.

"I mentioned your birthday to Dr. Chen a few days ago, and today he brought me this to give you. It must be a card."

"How thoughtful," Mom said. "I mentioned your birthday to Mrs. Chen, too, when we went to lunch last week. She probably went right out and got this for you."

"Thanks," Anna Mei said, her heart sinking a little as she took it. It seemed they never had a single conversation anymore that didn't involve the Chens.

"Well, aren't you going to open it?" her mother asked, after Dad had gone upstairs.

As if I had a choice, Anna Mei thought glumly. She slid her thumb under the envelope's flap. Inside was a smaller envelope, this one all red except for some bright gold Chinese lettering on the front. She opened it and found a folded note, along with a crisp five-dollar bill and three ones.

"So . . . they're giving me eight dollars?" Anna Mei asked. It seemed like a pretty unusual gift—in fact, it was downright weird.

"Maybe the note explains it," Mom suggested.

Anna Mei unfolded the note and immediately recognized Kai's small, neat handwriting. She read the words out loud:

Dear Anna Mei,

I tell my son Kai the words to say and he writes them for me, because my English writing is not good. Please accept this gift of hóng bao, which in China is given from older

people to younger people for good luck. You already have much luck, Anna Mei, being born during Chinese New Year in the Year of the Tiger. We are pleased to wish you also prosperity, happiness, and long life.

Mrs. Jinhai Chen

By the time she had finished, her mother was already typing something into the laptop. "*Hóng bao,*" she read from the screen. "Red envelopes that are given to children during Chinese New Year, usually containing money. Amounts vary but often include the number eight because it is considered lucky."

Anna Mei scanned the note again. Something in there had caught her eye the first time.

"I wonder how Mrs. Chen knew I was born during Chinese New Year," she said. "We learned in social studies that their New Year lasts for fifteen days, but the starting date is based on the phases of the moon. It can start anytime between the end of January and the middle of February."

"She must have looked up the New Year dates from the year you were born," Mom said. "That was so sweet of her. You'll have to send her a thank you note. Or better yet, come with me next time I visit so you can thank her in person."

Great, Anna Mei thought, watching her mother take some dinner rolls out of the freezer and put them on a baking tray. *First Dad wants me to be best friends with Kai, and now Mom thinks I should have tea with Mrs. Chen.*

"I know that Dad asked us to be nice to the Chens," she said, slipping the money and note back into the red envelope. "But I don't understand why you like them so much. Especially Mrs. Chen—she's nothing like you."

"What do you mean?" Mom asked. "Our husbands work together. Our kids go to the same school."

"Yeah, but she's so quiet and so . . . I don't know, sort of retro. The way she dresses, and how she waits on Dr. Chen and Kai—it's like she's a housewife from some kind of time warp."

"Well, you have to understand that Mrs. Chen was raised in a whole different culture than we were," Mom said, sliding the tray into the oven next to the casserole. "She's doing what she was taught to do— be a homemaker who makes things as comfortable as possible for her family. She takes pride in doing that well. Staying in the background is something she was taught, too. And on top of all that, there's the language barrier. Think how difficult it would be to go to a store or restaurant, knowing you'll probably have trouble understanding and being understood. I think she's pretty brave to face that in country after country, wherever her husband's work takes her."

Okay, even though *brave* wasn't exactly a word Anna Mei would have used to describe timid Mrs. Chen, she could see her mother's point. But right now she was trying to make one of her own. "I still don't see what you have in common with her, Mom. You went to college and have an important job at the hospital. All she does is stay home all day. I'd never want to be like that."

Her mother came back and sat down again. "Anna Mei, you're too young to understand this yet," she said, "but figuring out what's best for your family is one of the hardest parts of being a parent. No matter what choice you make, there are always consequences to consider. In a lot of ways I admire Mrs. Chen for devoting so much time and energy to her husband and son. Sometimes I wish I could do that, too."

"You mean, instead of being a nurse?" Anna Mei asked. In a conversation full of surprises, this was the biggest one so far.

Mom nodded. "You know that I love nursing, Anna Mei, but lately I've felt like my job is taking too much time away from our family life. In a few years you really *will* be getting your driver's license, and then college won't be far behind. Mrs. Chen and I were talking about that just the other day."

Talking about it the other day? Great, now Mom's having heart-to-hearts with Mrs. Chen about me. What's next—inviting Mrs. Chen over to give me cooking lessons?

It was probably a good thing that the oven timer rang then, leaving Anna Mei's question unasked.

Chapter Twenty-Three

8,000 Miles Away

After a whole weekend of celebrating her birthday, Anna Mei woke up Monday morning worried about all the study time she'd missed.

She had planned to really get some work done on Sunday night, after Aunt Karen's family left. But then Lauren—her best friend from Boston—called to wish her a happy birthday, and they ended up talking for over an hour. Then she realized she'd forgotten to bring home her English book, so she had to call Zandra to get the assignment. But Zandra wasn't exactly in a hurry to get off the phone, either, and the next thing Anna Mei knew, it was too late to do much of anything.

So on Monday night, while Dad was cleaning up after dinner, she dumped her backpack out on her bed and settled in for a marathon homework session. Her biggest worry was the unit test coming up in social studies class. Mr. Crandall had said it would cover what they'd been learning about Asia for the past few months.

As she started to review those chapters from the beginning, Anna Mei remembered her father flipping through her book back in October, stopping to point out the section about China. It was funny—having been there himself twelve years ago, meeting the people and experiencing the culture firsthand, he felt more of an attachment to China than she did. And really, she hadn't expected anything in this class to change that.

But now as she started turning the pages one by one, it dawned on her that all the people in the pictures looked a lot like her. In her world, most people didn't. She could remember a few Chinese families in the suburban neighborhood where she'd grown up, and there had been other Chinese kids at her grade school, but she hadn't been close to any of them. Back then she'd only been interested in her own group of friends.

Her parents did take her to Boston's Chinatown a couple of times when she was little. Anna Mei remembered passing through the huge gate with its bright green roof and lion statues. Inside were rows and rows of flower shops, fruit stands, teahouses, and stores full of painted dishes and embroidered slippers. Feeling overwhelmed and confused by all the noise, the crowds, and the strange-sounding languages, she wasn't sorry when it was time to leave.

Anna Mei wondered how she would feel if she went there now. This time of year they would be having their annual Chinese New Year celebration. She'd never been interested in things like that before, hadn't felt any connection to them. She'd been much more excited about seeing the site of the Boston Tea Party, and other places that were important in American history.

But now, sitting in a room some 8,000 miles from the place she'd been born, Anna Mei found herself drawn to the images in the book, especially the ones of women. Some showed them dressed in modern western clothing, hurrying along crowded city streets framed by high-rises. Others showed women wearing loose-fitting pants and huge straw hats, working in their homes or on farms.

One of them could be my birth mother, Anna Mei found herself thinking. *I wonder where she is now, and what her life is like. I hope God has blessed her the way he's blessed me.*

Cleo, who'd been curled up in a furry ball on the bed, yawned and stretched, then came over to push her head against Anna Mei's hand. Taking her eyes off the page seemed to break her train of thought. She shook her head to clear it.

"Okay, but just for a minute," she said, letting Cleo climb into her lap. "We've got a long night of studying ahead of us."

Chapter Twenty-Four

Universe-2

As she did every Tuesday, Anna Mei raced to the lunchroom to spend time with her friends. She knew that Luis was home with a sore throat, but she was looking forward to talking more with Danny and Zandra about the planetarium show they'd seen on her birthday.

She and Zandra got there first and claimed their usual table. But when Danny arrived a few minutes later, he wasn't alone—Kai was with him.

"Hi!" Zandra greeted them, her smile as friendly as always. "We were just talking about you."

"Naturally," Danny said, taking one of the empty chairs and pushing the other toward Kai. "No one can talk about anything else when I'm in the room. I'm used to it by now."

"Wow, another lunch from home?" Anna Mei asked, seeing him take a paper bag from his backpack. Amazingly, he had been bringing his own lunches lately instead of buying them.

"Coach is making us cut out the junk food and empty calories," Danny explained. "We've got to stay lean and mean. Right, Kai? Besides, I can't let this kid keep beating me in the backstroke. It's bad for my self-esteem."

Zandra laughed. "Somehow I don't think self-esteem will ever be a problem for you," she said. "But swimming is what Anna Mei and I were just talking about—we're planning to go to your meet on Saturday."

"Hey, great!" Danny said, pulling a sandwich and an orange out of his lunch bag. "With both of you there, plus the parents who come, our fans will be in the dozens."

"Well, I said I would *try* to go, remember?" Anna Mei said. "I'm not sure yet."

"Oh, come on," Zandra said. "You can take a break from homework for a couple of hours. It's for a good cause."

Ugh. Now Kai will think all I do is sit around the house and study, trying to keep up with him. Thanks, Zandra.

"Actually, I'll need to do some studying, too, to get ready for that social studies test," Danny said. "If I know Mr. Crandall, it's going to be a hard one."

Kai had been quietly eating his own lunch from home, having given up on cafeteria food after his first day here. "If you like, we could study together after the swim meet is over," he offered.

"Really?" Danny asked. "That would be great—for me, anyway. I'm guessing this particular test won't be much of a challenge for you."

Kai shrugged, his mouth turning up in a half-smile. "China is a vast country," he said. "There is always more to learn."

That struck Anna Mei as an interesting thought. It seemed like Kai knew everything about everything, but of course that couldn't be true.

"Like what?" she asked him, pulling the lid off her yogurt. "What else would you like to learn about China?"

Instead of answering the question, he asked her one, "Why do you wish to know that?"

"I'm just curious," she told him.

He turned to look at her then, not smiling the way he did at Danny, but with that expression he always seemed to have when he talked to her. It made her feel as if he was on the verge of accusing her of something.

"Curious?" he repeated. "I am very surprised to hear that, Anna Mei. Since living here I have talked often about Chinese language, culture, history, athletics. Yet, you have not shown interest in any of it."

Anna Mei opened her mouth and then shut it again. Nothing she could she possibly say would express what she was feeling anyway. What she really wanted to do was throw something, kick the table over, yell at him—*anything* to knock that arrogant look off his face. Who did he think he was, coming into *her* school, sitting here with *her* friends, talking to her like *that*?

"You know what? Never mind," she said, quickly shoving the rest of her lunch back in her bag. "I'm supposed to help Miss Haynes with something before science class, so I need to get going. See you guys later."

She took off without looking at any of them. If Danny and Zandra thought Kai was such a great kid, they were welcome to him, today and every day from now on.

It took just over twenty-four hours for Anna Mei to discover an important fact: deciding she would never speak to Kai Chen again was one thing, while *actually* never speaking to him again was another. On Wednesday the whole universe seemed to rise up in some kind of crazy conspiracy to put him directly in her path.

Miss Haynes started things off. At the end of the Science Club meeting, she explained that while team members were expected to be knowledgeable about every topic, Quest rules specified that two team members would compete in each category. Therefore, starting next week, the sixteen-person team would be divided into eight teams of two, based on their areas of expertise. Oh, and the team T-shirts she had ordered should arrive any day now—wasn't that exciting?

Anna Mei sank down in her chair, closing her eyes and trying to take deep breaths. Even before Miss Haynes announced the teams, she knew she would be paired with Kai. That meant that in addition to presenting their own projects on biofuels and carbon sinks, the two of them would represent the whole team on any questions about plants.

I don't care—no one can make me study with him, she thought. *I don't even want to be in the same room with him. We'll just have to get ready for the Science Quest separately.*

She didn't feel the need to tell Miss Haynes that. She would have to tell Kai, eventually, but for today the best she could do was get herself out to the parking lot and into her father's car without completely losing it.

As it turned out, thinking of the car as some kind of safe zone proved to be another delusion. On the drive home, Dad shared the news that the Chens had invited them to dinner at a nice restaurant on Sunday afternoon, as a way of repaying the hospitality the Andersons had shown them.

"Not that it's necessary, of course," Dad said, turning onto their street. "But it's a very nice gesture. I know Kai isn't your favorite person, but I'm sure that with all of us there it will be a pleasant cultural experience."

Anna Mei closed her eyes again. Now Dad was starting to sound just like Dr. Chen, talking about "cultural experiences." She knew that short of coming down with the bubonic plague in the next few days, there was no way for her to get out of going to that dinner. By her count, the score was now Universe–2, Anna Mei–0.

Chapter Twenty-Five

The Jade Garden

She ended up skipping the swim meet on Saturday, telling Zandra she had family obligations. It wasn't exactly true, but having to be with the Chens on Sunday was bad enough—she wasn't going anywhere near them on Saturday.

The dinner reservation at The Jade Garden, a popular Chinese restaurant near the university, was for four o'clock. Although the Andersons arrived a few minutes early, the Chens were already waiting in the large red and black lobby.

Anna Mei had spent the past few days working out strategies for how to get through this. Her first trick was managing to get seated between her mother and Mrs. Chen. That way she could talk mostly to Mom, who was less likely than Dad to say something embarrassing. And she could pretty much avoid Kai all together, since he was safely on the other side of *his* mother.

Dr. Chen insisted on pointing out his favorite dishes on the menu, which Anna Mei found obnoxious, although everyone else seemed to appreciate it. Then he ordered for his whole family—in Mandarin, no less.

Anna Mei gritted her teeth and ordered something she knew she liked—orange chicken with fried rice and an eggroll. The server was a pretty Chinese woman, probably a college student judging by her age. Her jet black hair was pulled into a long braid, and she wore a silky green *qipao*—the traditional Chinese gown with high collar and cap sleeves. Anna Mei had a similar one, in pink, hanging in her closet. Her parents bought it for her in Changsha, right before they took her home with them. She had never pictured herself actually wearing it, but this young woman looked beautiful in hers.

A few minutes later the server brought out bowls of steaming hot egg drop soup. It wasn't Anna Mei's favorite but she took a few sips anyway, wanting to appear too busy for conversation.

When the entrées arrived they were served with chopsticks. Dr. Chen offered to give a demonstration, but Mom and Dad said they had learned the art of using chopsticks on their trip to China, and brushed up while visiting Seattle last summer. Anna Mei was the only one to use the knife and fork that were already on the table.

Concentrating on her food, she let the conversation swirl around her. Dad and Dr. Chen were discussing their upcoming field trip to the University of Wisconsin, a partner in the Great Lakes Bioenergy project. Mom and Mrs. Chen talked about the art show they'd seen a few weeks ago. With any luck at all no one would—

"Yes, Father," she heard Kai saying, in answer to something Dr. Chen had asked him. "The first competition will be held in March, at a school near here. Only teams that win first, second, and third place will move to the next level, to compete with students from the entire state."

Dr. Chen smiled and clapped a hand on Dad's shoulder. "We can be certain that Westside School will advance. With my son and your daughter on the team, there can be no doubt about that!"

As all the adults chimed in enthusiastically, Anna Mei found herself smiling through gritted teeth again. This situation was exactly what the phrase *rubbing salt in the wound* was invented for.

She was grateful when the server returned to clear away the plates. That meant the check would be arriving next, which Dr. Chen would probably make a big show of accepting. Then this day she'd been dreading would be over, and she'd be back at home with her own family, where she belonged.

"And who would care for some dessert today?" the server asked. "We offer a delicious selection of egg custard tarts, sponge cakes, and steamed fruit."

Dessert. Ugh.

"These fruits," Mrs. Chen said, "they are cooked with honey?"

The server nodded. "Oh yes, all our food is served in the traditional style."

"Honeyed fruit is my son's favorite," Mrs. Chen happily confided. "Please bring a dish for him."

"Of course," the server said, jotting down the order. "And will your daughter be having some, too?"

The question was so unexpected that it took a minute to sink in. But when it did, Anna Mei felt her face flush as bright as the scarlet wall hangings draped around the room. Through that red fog she heard Dr. Chen laugh.

That did it. She was not going to sit there and be *laughed* at. She pushed her chair back and stood up, almost crashing into the server who was still standing there.

"I don't see why that's so funny," Anna Mei heard herself say in a choked voice she barely recognized. "I'm *not* your daughter. I'm nothing like you—any of you!"

Whether she would have said more, she'd never know, since one glance around the table revealed her father's shocked face and her mother's sad one. Both were like stab wounds to a heart that was already sore.

She turned and ran then, out of the dining room, through the lobby and into the small, glassed-in entryway that stood between the lobby and the parking lot. It was freezing in there, and she hadn't stopped to grab her coat. But she had no choice—she couldn't go back inside, and she couldn't get into the locked car. She had no other place to go.

Her parents found her there a few minutes later, her cheek pressed up against the cold glass.

"Anna Mei—" her mother started, but Anna Mei stopped her.

"Please, Mom," she said, her voice thick with the tears she was trying hard to hold back. "I don't . . . I just can't. . . . Can we please just go home now?"

Her father put her coat over her shoulders, then the three of them got into the car and drove home in silence.

Chapter Twenty-Six

Where We Found You

At home, Anna Mei apologized to her parents for causing a scene, and promised to apologize to the Chens, too. But for now, she told them, she needed to be alone for a while. They exchanged one of those parental glances, the kind that meant *what do you think?*, before telling her she could go on up to her room.

She tried to take her mind off the whole thing by studying for tomorrow's social studies test. But that ended up making her feel even worse. The same images of China that had intrigued her just a few days ago now seemed to mock her. After an hour of getting nowhere, she decided to give up on the whole thing and get ready for bed.

She'd just brushed her teeth and changed into

her pajamas when her father knocked on the bedroom door. "I think we should talk for a few minutes, Anna Mei."

Climbing into bed, she sat back against a pillow and braced herself for the lecture she figured was coming. When he opened the door she thought his face looked drawn and tired. It made her feel even worse to know that she was responsible.

"I really am sorry, Dad," she told him again, as he sat down in the chair by the window and Cleo snuggled up beside her. "And don't worry—I'll apologize to the Chens, too."

"Right now the only thing I'm worried about is you," he said. "Your mother and I can't understand what came over you tonight. The server just made an honest mistake, that's all. She thought—"

"I know," Anna Mei said, in a tiny voice that seemed completely unrelated to the one she'd used in the restaurant.

"Then why did it upset you so much? Have the Chens done something to make you angry?"

An answer jumped into her head, *Yes—they came here*.

She stopped herself from saying it, though. It would make her sound like a little kid, upset because someone else wanted to play in her sand box. That wouldn't help her father to understand how being around them made her feel.

"It's not anything they've *done*," she told him. "It's

just that I don't want people thinking I belong with them instead of with you and Mom. I don't like being reminded all the time that I'm different from you."

He frowned, his forehead wrinkling above his glasses. "I thought we worked through this last year, when you did that heritage report," he finally said. "You said that being adopted didn't bother you, and that being in our family was where you belonged."

She remembered the relief she felt back then, when she'd finally confided her feelings to her parents, and they helped her realize that looks had nothing to do with belonging. No matter where she had been born, no matter how she looked, she was *their* daughter—she was Anna Mei Anderson.

The problem now was that it seemed like no one *else* got that.

"It *doesn't* bother me that I was adopted," she said, keeping her eyes fixed on Cleo's sleeping face instead of Dad's worried one. "But ever since the Chens got here, it seems like everyone thinks I should be interested in knowing all about China, as if that's the most important thing about me. And it just . . . isn't."

He considered this for a moment before answering, but when he spoke, his voice was low and reassuring. "All right, I can understand that, and I'm sorry if it seems like we've been pushing you into something that makes you uncomfortable. That wasn't our intention. We just thought that getting to know the Chens would help give you something that your mom and I can't. You may not care much about China, Anna Mei, but it means a lot to us. It's where we found *you*."

He stood up and came over to the bed, then reached out to cover her hand with his large, strong one. "The last thing your mom and I wanted to do was upset you, especially to the point where you'd lash out like that. We've always left it up to you to decide how much you wanted to learn about where you came from. That's not going to change now, even with the Chens here. All right?"

She nodded, not trusting herself to speak.

Dad bent down and kissed the top of her head. "You get some sleep now. Things always look better in the morning, as my father used to tell me."

"Okay, Dad," she said. "And . . . thanks."

After he'd gone, turning off the light behind him, she pulled up the covers and waited for sleep to come. But even with her father's words of reassurance in her head, she lay awake for a while thinking about what had happened in the restaurant. She found herself wishing she could turn back the clock and start over again. In her alternate scenario, Anna Mei imagined herself calmly explaining to the server that she was not the Chens' daughter, and that she didn't care for any steamed fruit, thank you. The things she had *actually* said—and the public scene she'd made— were so unlike her that she could hardly believe they had happened. *Where did all that come from?*

She tossed and turned, wondering how she could bear to face Kai in the morning. Seeing him in her classes would be bad enough, she realized, but having to work with him on the Science Quest team would be pretty much impossible. Not only would she be miserable the whole time, but there was no way she could put her best effort into the competition. And that wouldn't be fair to the rest of the team.

The only thing to do, she decided, was to quit Science Club altogether. Miss Haynes would be disappointed, but Kai was a strong competitor—she could pair him up with any of the alternates and they would do well.

I won't wait until the club meeting on Wednesday, she thought. *I'll tell Miss Haynes after school tomorrow.*

She slept a little after that, but it was a restless sleep, filled with anxious dreams.

Chapter Twenty-Seven

Not Very Funny

Monday was gray, bitterly cold, and never-ending. Anna Mei dragged herself from class to class, spending what little energy she had on keeping her distance from Kai. She skipped lunch, telling Zandra she needed to study for her social studies test. That at least was true—everything she had learned in that class over the past few months seemed to have evaporated from her brain.

By the last period of the day, when Mr. Crandall handed out the tests, her head felt like it weighed a hundred pounds. Her eyes kept trying to close without her permission. As she struggled to fill in some answers, the whole thing seemed to pass in a blur.

Danny came up to her afterward, looking worried. "Are you okay?" he asked.

It was like an echo of the time he'd asked her that last fall. Then he'd been able to convince her that she didn't need to try so hard to be perfect. Of course, that was before Kai Chen had come to town and showed her what "perfect" really meant.

"Honestly, Danny, I don't feel very well," she admitted. "I have . . . a lot on my mind today. I really want to talk with you about it but right now I'm supposed to meet with Miss Haynes, and you have to get to swim practice. I'll call you tonight, okay?"

It was getting late, so she hurried to the science room without stopping at her locker. She knew she would need all her courage to do this. She had loved being in the club, especially after she qualified for Science Quest. And Miss Haynes would be pretty unhappy about it, too, not to mention her father.

From this jumble of thoughts, a prayer took shape in her mind. *Dear God, please give me the strength to get through this day. I already have a lot of people mad at me, and I'm about to add to that list. Please help them to see that I'm trying my best to do what's right.*

The door to Miss Haynes's room was already open. Anna Mei went in without knocking, expecting to see her teacher already there. Instead she saw the one person she would have traveled to Timbuktu to avoid—Kai Chen.

Anna Mei's shoulders sagged under the weight of it all.

Okay, am I somehow the punch line in someone

else's joke? she wondered, wearily. *Because it's not very funny.*

"I am waiting for Miss Haynes," Kai said, seeming just as surprised as she was. "Has she been delayed?"

"I'm not . . . I don't know," she said. "She told me to meet her here after school."

They both stood there for a moment, not moving. In the uncomfortable silence, Anna Mei felt tempted to turn and walk out. But she hated to put off her meeting with Miss Haynes, now that her mind was made up about Science Club.

Besides, even though she hadn't wanted to deal with Kai today, maybe it wouldn't be such a bad idea to go ahead and get the apology over with. It would be nice to be able to tell her parents that she'd already taken care of it—one Chen down and two to go.

"Listen, Kai," she said, "as long as you're here, I think you should know that . . . I wanted to tell you that . . ."

Come on—just say it!

She took a breath and forced the words out all at once. "I'm really sorry for what I said at the restaurant yesterday. To your parents, I mean. It was out of line and I shouldn't have done it."

There—now all he had to do was accept and go on his way. Shouldn't he be at swim practice anyway?

But of course nothing with Kai could be that simple. He stood there, his head tilted, looking at her. Then just when she'd decided to forget the whole thing, he suddenly swung his backpack onto one of the tables and sat down next to it.

"That is a very interesting apology," he said. "You are sorry for saying something, but you are not sorry for believing it."

She frowned, trying to work this out. Of course, that was the usual scenario where Kai was concerned. "Look, all I'm trying to say—"

"I know—that you are nothing like us," Kai finished for her. "It may have been a surprise for my parents to hear, but not for me. You have already shown me your low opinion of my family."

"My low opinion?" she repeated. Then, just to make sure she'd heard him right: "*My* low opinion?"

He just looked at her with that calm gaze of his, the one that always seemed to make her so furious. It was doing the trick now, too.

"Kai Chen, I can't believe you just said that to me! Ever since you got here you've been letting me know that nothing about me or this school, or even this town, is good enough for you. When I first heard you were coming, I actually felt sorry for you. What a joke that was!"

"Sorry for me?" This, at least, seemed to surprise him. "Why?"

"Because *I* was new here once," she said. "*I* was the new kid, the one with the weird name who didn't fit in. It took me a long time to feel comfortable and to start making friends. But you—you just came walking in all full of yourself, Mister Been-Everywhere-and-Seen-Everything. You have so much self-confidence it could fill a football stadium."

How could she have felt so tired just a few minutes ago? Now she felt energized, wound up, raring to go. He had asked for it and he was going to hear it—all of it.

"So imagine how silly I felt, thinking I was going to help you make friends and try to fit in here. As if you were interested in fitting in with a bunch of small-town hicks! Plus you never missed a single chance to let me know that I wasn't smart enough, and that I didn't know anything about China, even though I was born there. Now you sit here and tell me that *I* have a low opinion of *you*? It's . . . unbelievable."

She'd been pacing around the room as she talked, but now she stopped, wondering if her words were getting through at all. She could never tell with Kai—since he rarely smiled and never raised his voice, it was hard to know what he was thinking.

When he did answer, it was in the same even voice he always used. Only his words were surprising. "When I first arrived in this place, I spoke too harshly to you about your school and your town. Please understand that it was my own unhappiness that made me do this."

Chapter Twenty-Eight

"Exceptional"

Okay, now *she* needed to sit down. This was by far the most personal thing Kai had ever said to her.

"Well, I guess I can see that," she admitted, dropping her backpack on the floor and sinking into a chair across from him. "I wasn't exactly thrilled when I first moved here, either. In fact, I was pretty upset about the whole thing."

He nodded. "For me there was great disappointment in coming here. This is my father's first assignment in the United States. Naturally I was excited. I wanted to live in one of the big cities I had read about—Los Angeles or New York or maybe Washington, D.C."

"So what did he say when you told him that?"

"*Told* him? Where we live is my father's choice," he said. "My duty is to respect his wishes, not question them."

Of course Anna Mei knew that the Chens were pretty traditional, but this sounded extreme.

"You mean, you don't get any say in where you live? Ever?"

"A Chinese father is the head of his family," he explained. "My father makes decisions that are best for my mother and me. Wherever he says we must go, we go."

"No wonder you were upset when you ended up here," she said. "It's nothing like what you'd hoped."

His mouth quirked in a half-smile. "That is what you would call an understatement," he said. "But soon my feelings changed. I learned that the teachers and students here are very friendly, Anna Mei. They welcomed me with kindness. I have attended more than fifteen schools, and I have learned that this is not always the way."

She almost gasped at that. "Fifteen! I can't imagine that. It must be so hard to be the new kid all the time."

"Something I have learned from being at many schools is this: what others think about me is not important. I do not waste time worrying about it. Maybe this is what you mean by self-confidence. At every school I am Kai Chen, always the same. Some people will like this and others will not. Either way,

I will be there for a little while and then I will be gone."

When this day started, the last thing Anna Mei had expected to feel was sympathy for Kai. For weeks she had been longing for the day his family would pack up and move on, never giving a thought to how that might feel from his point of view. Now she found herself wanting to cheer him up somehow.

"But you get to see so many interesting places, and do such exciting things," she reminded him.

"My father thinks it is very important for me to have cultural experiences. He keeps a list of these on his computer." Then he smiled—a full-on, all-out smile. "I am lucky that many of them are also fun."

"And he's very proud of you," Anna Mei pointed out, surprising herself again. Now she was defending stuffy old Dr. Chen, of all people. "He's always talking about how smart you are."

As quickly as it had come, the smile seemed to disappear. Kai slid off the table and walked over to the window, where he stood watching a fresh snowfall cover up the footprints in the courtyard.

"When I was born, my father named me Kai Hao, which means *exceptional*," he said, still not looking at her. "Because *his* father could not provide many advantages, my father's success was the result of his own hard work. He wishes for his son to achieve even greater success. To do this I must study for many hours and learn all that I can."

The wistful tone in Kai's voice made her feel a little sad. She'd been thinking that he was some kind of genius, just showing off to the teachers and the other kids. She had practically been killing herself to keep up, resenting his success because it seemed to come so easily. The truth was that Kai was a dedicated student who worked very hard at everything he did, all while under constant pressure to be *exceptional*.

"I'm sure he just wants what's best for you," she told him. "I mean, fathers don't always get it right—mine still thinks of me as a seven-year-old sometimes. But it's nice that they care so much."

"Please understand," he said, turning away from the window to face her again. "In my culture, it is expected that parents choose the path for their children to follow. Being a dutiful and respectful son is not a burden—it shows that I am grateful for my parents' devotion to me."

Chapter Twenty-Nine

Chinese Chinese

Talking about his parents reminded Anna Mei what had started this whole conversation.

"I really am sorry about what happened at The Jade Garden," she told him. "When I said I wasn't like them, I only meant that I don't think of myself as being Chinese. At least, not in the way all of *you* are."

"So you are Chinese . . . but also not Chinese?"

She had to smile at that—it sounded so goofy. "I don't know, Kai, it's something I haven't really sorted out for myself, I guess. Of course I've known my whole life that I was adopted, and that my birth parents were Chinese. But that didn't really mean anything to me. My life was in Boston, with my family and my friends."

"Then when I was eleven, we moved here. I was worried that being Chinese made me too different, and I didn't want to be different. After a while I realized that no one really cared what country I was born in, so I went back to not thinking about it much. Until . . . your family moved to town."

"An actual *Chinese* Chinese family," Kai said.

That made her laugh out loud. "Well, you *are*," she said. "And every time any of you said something about China, it reminded me that I don't really know anything about it."

"This was a surprise to me when I met you," he admitted. "In China our ancestry and culture are of great importance."

"I'm not saying it was right," she said. "I realize now that even though being Chinese isn't *everything* I am, it is *part* of who I am. I hate to admit it, but maybe you've been right about that all along."

He smiled that genuine smile again. "I am glad to hear that I am right about something. You have never said this before. And I am glad you came into the room today instead of Miss Haynes."

Miss Haynes! Anna Mei had almost forgotten why she'd come here.

"That's weird—she was supposed to meet me here half an hour ago," she said, picking up her backpack. "But I guess I don't need to see her today after all. What about you?"

"My intention was to tell Miss Haynes that I could not participate in the science competition."

She swung around to look at him. "*What?*" she said, her voice shrill enough to frighten small animals. "You're dropping out of the Quest? Why?"

He looked a little surprised by her strong reaction. Then he shrugged. "It was my father's wish that I join your group," he said. "He asked that I choose a project in the field of biochemistry, to follow in his footsteps. This was never my own wish."

"Well then, won't he be upset if you quit?"

"He will," Kai admitted. "But that is not the important question. The important question is this— why did *you* join Science Club, Anna Mei?"

She couldn't imagine what that had to do with Kai or his father, but at least it was easy to answer. "Because I love science," she said simply.

"Exactly," he said, sounding like a scientist who'd just proven his hypothesis. "So you did not join because it was expected of you. You did not choose a biofuel experiment because that is what your father wanted. You did these things because of your love for science. That makes you an essential component of the team. In other words, irreplaceable."

She shook her head. "I still don't see what that has to do with *you* quitting."

"But it's very simple," he insisted. "It was clear to me that my participation on the team could affect your attitude and performance in the competition. The replaceable one needed to be replaced. This is what I came to tell Miss Haynes."

Finally, Anna Mei could see a glimmer of light at the end of this twisty tunnel. "So you're saying that since we weren't getting along, you decided to drop out of the competition—for the good of the team."

"Exactly," he said again, then looked mystified as she started to laugh. "Why is that funny?"

"I'll tell you," she said, still laughing as they headed out the door, "but you're never going to believe it!"

Chapter Thirty

Time for Tea

All dressed up and sitting on the couch in the Chens' immaculate living room, Anna Mei carefully stirred the hot, fragrant tea in her delicate cup.

Okay, this isn't as bad as I thought it would be, she decided. *As long I don't spill anything on the rug, that is.*

She had been nervous about this day ever since her mother suggested it. Her first choice would have been to apologize to the Chens on neutral turf—maybe in a different restaurant where she could offer to treat *them.* But Mom reminded her that Mrs. Chen had been inviting her for weeks now. And because it was Saturday, Dr. Chen would be there as well. It was a perfect opportunity.

It hadn't been easy, telling them how sorry she was for her outburst at The Jade Garden. But both of them had been gracious and forgiving. Mrs. Chen had even taken Anna Mei's hands in her own, the way Grandmother Anna used to do.

"Such a sweet girl," she said, in her gentle voice. "Come now and join me for tea and *dim sum*."

So while Dr. Chen and Kai headed off to Kai's swim meet, Anna Mei and her mother stayed for tea, served from a red and white pot made of bone china. A round platter filled with tiny pieces of water chestnut cake sat on the glossy coffee table.

The house was in the nicest part of town, surrounded by other stately, historic homes. Anna Mei knew the Chens were only renting it, and that the expensive furniture and thick rugs probably belonged to the owners. Scattered around the room, though, were many decorative art pieces, most of them Asian.

"Are all these yours, Mrs. Chen?" she asked, pointing out a display of carved figurines on a shelf.

Mrs. Chen smiled and nodded. "I have collected these pieces for many years. I bring some wherever I go, so that every place feels a little like my home in Beijing."

"So you have your own house there?" Anna Mei asked.

"Oh, yes," Mrs. Chen said. "Sometimes my husband has work in Beijing. Sometimes he does not work for several months. Then we go home."

"And you have other family there?" Anna Mei asked, realizing that she'd never asked Kai about his grandparents, aunts, uncles, and cousins.

She caught her mother's warning glance, but it was too late. A tiny frown replaced the warm smile on Mrs. Chen's face.

"This is another way I see that you are lucky, Anna Mei," she said. "I see your family, gathered for feasting and celebration—elders for wisdom, young children for joy. Your mother and her sister, cooking food together with much laughter, like my sister and me."

Anna Mei was confused—she had asked about Mrs. Chen's family, not her own. But at least now she knew that Kai had an aunt.

"Does your sister live in Beijing, too?" she asked.

This time a shadow seemed to pass over Mrs. Chen's face, and her hand shook a little as she set her teacup on the table.

"I will tell you, Anna Mei," she said, settling back in her chair. "And you, Margaret. Then you will both know the story of my beautiful sister, Mingyu."

For the next half hour, Anna Mei barely moved, listening to Mrs. Chen's soft, musical voice as she talked about growing up in the Chinese countryside with her sister. Like Mom and Aunt Karen, the two girls were very close. As the older one, Mingyu was often put in charge of little Lian while their parents worked in the fields. It was a quiet life but a happy one.

Then, when the girls were fifteen and seventeen, some excitement came into their lives. A neighboring family invited them to attend an all-day festival in the nearby city. The neighbors would act as chaperones. Lian—the shyer, quieter sister—would have preferred to stay at home, but Mingyu was full of sparkle and curiosity. She begged her parents until they agreed the girls could go.

At the festival they saw a puppet show, listened to a band concert, and watched the fireworks. Because she had never experienced anything like this in the countryside, Lian was frightened by the noise and the crowds. She never let go of her big sister's hand. She was relieved when one of the chaperones suggested a boat ride on the river, to escape the crowds. By now it was dark, and the moonlight made silver streaks on the black water. From that boat, Lian thought the whole world looked lovely and peaceful.

But the peacefulness did not last. Two men on the boat began to argue and shout. Soon they were fighting, their fists reaching out to strike each other. People rushed to get out of the way, and in the commotion, the boat tipped over. Cold water rushed up over Lian's head and pulled at her clothes, but she fought against it until she broke the surface. Everywhere people were crying out, and Lian began to cry out, too, calling Mingyu's name over and over again. Mingyu was the big sister, the strong one, the one who took care of her—surely she would conquer the river. But Mingyu did not answer.

Finally someone reached out and pulled Lian into a boat. Wet, shivering, and frightened, she stayed on the shore all through the night, hoping against hope that Mingyu would come. As terrible as that night was, worse was going home to her parents the next day without her sister. All three of them were heartbroken from the loss of their sparkling Mingyu. Lian was sure she would never feel happiness again.

Chapter Thirty-One

A Treasure

Anna Mei felt herself blinking back tears as Mrs. Chen finished. It almost felt like waking up from a dream—even with her less-than-perfect English, Mrs. Chen had made the story come alive.

"I'm so sorry, Lian," she heard her mother say, in a voice that sounded a little huskier than usual. "My sister Karen means the world to me, just as your sister did to you."

Mrs. Chen nodded. "This is why I think you should know the story, so that you understand. A family is a treasure, not to be taken for granted. I have only my husband and son now, but I understand their great value."

Anna Mei took a napkin from the table and used it to wipe her eyes.

"You think this is a sad story, Anna Mei?" Mrs. Chen said. "In some ways it is a happy one. When I feel sad or alone, I think of my sister's strength. I think of her light. In this way Mingyu still helps me. So in this way she is still alive."

Anna Mei just nodded, not trusting herself to speak.

"It's a beautiful story," Mom said. "Thank you for telling us."

"Ah, but it is not finished yet," Mrs. Chen said, getting up to refill their cups. When she settled into her chair again, Anna Mei thought she saw a sparkle in her eyes. "I will tell you the rest now."

Mrs. Chen picked up the story where she had left off. She and her parents, living on the farm with their work and their grief, were surprised several years later by a visit from a handsome young man. He was very polite and very kind, explaining that he had been on the riverbank that terrible night of the accident. When he saw the boat tip over, he hurried to find another boat so he could help the people still in the water. One of those people, he said, was Lian.

He told her that he had never forgotten her pale face in the moonlight. From a distance, he had watched over her until morning, wanting to be sure that no harm came to her while she kept vigil for her sister. For the past few years he had been attending a university, but after graduating, he made up his mind that he would try to find Lian. He wanted to see again the girl who had shown such courage—even when all hope was gone, she did not give up. This was someone, he thought, who could stand by his side always.

"So of course you have guessed about this man," Mrs. Chen said, a smile lighting her face. "This man who came a long way over the hills and out of the past, looking for a bride."

Anna Mei gasped. "Dr. Chen?"

Mrs. Chen laughed, a sound as musical as bells ringing. "I see you are surprised," she said. "You think of my husband only as a scientist, a man with gray in his hair. But when he was a young man, Jinhai Chen reached out to save me. Then later he came to the farm to find me again. I thought to myself that day, it was my Mingyu that brought him to me."

She came over and took Anna Mei's hands again. "When I see you, Anna Mei, I think of my beautiful sister. There is brightness inside you that is like hers. And now I have shared her story with you. Now you know what Mingyu has shown me—in the darkness, a light can shine, turning great sorrow into great joy."

Anna Mei knew she would never forget the haunting story Mrs. Chen had told her. She couldn't believe she had ever thought of Kai's mother as a timid housewife without any purpose or direction in her life. The truth was that Mrs. Chen was a wise and strong woman, someone who supported and served her husband not because it was expected of her, but because she loved him with all her heart.

She realized she had been wrong about Dr. Chen, too. She had always thought of him as extremely serious and formal, a person who talked mostly about his work, when he wasn't bragging about his son. Yet this man had jumped into a rescue boat the moment he saw a group of strangers in trouble. This man had followed his heart halfway across the Chinese countryside, looking for a woman he didn't even know yet.

Now Anna Mei thought she understood why they both poured all their energy, their care, their hopes and dreams into their son. Having lived through poverty and heartache, they wanted him to grow up well-educated, safe, and secure. Their hopes for Kai were no different than what all parents hope for their children.

All the time she had been thinking of the Chens as uninteresting—even irrelevant—she'd been missing who they really were. Now she wondered what else she'd been missing every time they had tried to share something with her, only to have her turn away.

Of course, the same was true with how she'd seen Kai. When it came to misjudging people and pushing them away, his name belonged at the top of her list. All her jealousy, all her competiveness, all her frustration—it just added up to a whole lot of nothing.

Not that Kai would have been easy to get know. He had learned long ago how to protect himself by not getting too close to anyone. But she should have at least tried. And now that Kai's protective shell had been cracked open a little, Anna Mei hoped to convince him that taking the time to get to know someone—to make a friend now and then—was worthwhile.

After all, they'd have to spend a lot of time together practicing for Science Quest. And of course there was lunch period, where a table of four friends could always squeeze over and make room for five.

Chapter Thirty-Two

Everything I Am

For the next three weeks, Anna Mei spent as much time as she could working on her display board and practicing for the regional competition. But that didn't mean driving herself crazy, like she did before. The days of running frantically from project to project were behind her for good. After all, the reason she had joined Science Club in the first place was to have fun—she figured it was about time she started having some.

Of course, having fun was a lot easier now that she and Kai were getting along. He'd come over to her house to study a few times, and even stayed for dinner the night her mother made a vegetarian lasagna.

"This is very good, Mrs. Anderson," he said, when she offered him a second helping. "In general I have not found American food to be so . . . appetizing."

"Well, technically, this is Italian food," Dad said, smiling. "But it was prepared by a pretty good American cook."

"My mother is also a very good cook," Kai told them. "That may be why I do not always enjoy other types of food. None are as delicious as those she makes for me."

"I've had some of your mother's cooking," Mom said, passing around a basket of garlic bread, "and I agree with you—it's wonderful. I'd love to try one of her recipes sometime."

Kai must have wasted no time sharing the compliment with his mother. The very next day, she called to invite both Anna Mei and her mother over for a Chinese cooking lesson. "This would be such a happy time for me," she told Mom, "like cooking again with my Mingyu."

"Sure, I'll go with you," Anna Mei said, looking up from her reading. Her mother had found her in the study, curled up with a book about the history of NASA. "I'd like to try to learn more about Chinese food than just how to order orange chicken and fried rice. Maybe she can even help me figure out which end of a chopstick is which."

Her mother smiled. "I'm glad," she said. "I remember when you told me that you wouldn't want to be anything like Mrs. Chen."

"It was true then," Anna Mei admitted. "And I didn't want to think that my birth mother might be like her, either. But now I feel like I'd be proud if she was."

"Does this mean you're ready to start learning more about your Chinese heritage?"

"I think so," she said, setting her book down on the table. "It feels a little like starting over, though. I mean, when we first moved here, I spent a lot time pretending to be someone I wasn't. I had to learn that it's always better to just be myself. But now I think I didn't really know who that was. I hadn't figured out how to be *everything* I am—both the 'Anna' *and* the 'Mei Li.'"

When Mom didn't answer right away, Anna Mei was afraid she'd said the wrong thing, or hurt her feelings somehow. Then her mother came over to sit on the ottoman at Anna Mei's feet. She laid one hand on Anna Mei's knee and used the other to wipe a tear from the corner of her eye.

"Anna Mei," she said, "you need to understand that nothing you could learn about yourself would make you any less our daughter." Then she smiled. "You're an Anderson, and that's never going to change."

"I'd never want it to," Anna Mei said, her throat tightening a little at the thought. "I'll always keep our family traditions, no matter what."

"And don't forget your faith, too—that's something else I'm happy we can share."

"It's kind of weird, isn't it?" Anna Mei asked. "If

you and Dad hadn't adopted me, I might not know what it's like to pray, or to trust that God has a plan for me. That's something Kai doesn't have."

"Well, you never know," Mom said. "Kai's experiences here, and the other places he goes, may teach him some things he hasn't thought about."

"I guess that's true," Anna Mei agreed. "I suppose the Chens could be learning things from us, just like we're learning from them."

"That brings me to another thing I wanted to talk to you about," Mom said. "It's time for me to make a change in my own life."

Mom explained that after thinking about it for a long time, and praying for guidance, she had decided to leave the hospital. She had just been offered a part-time nursing job at the university's clinical center. "The work might be less challenging," she said, "but I'll be home every night and some afternoons. I think it's worth the trade off. Besides, I can always go back to hospital work later."

"You mean when I'm grown and off to college," Anna Mei said, "in the not so distant future."

Her mother sighed. "Don't remind me," she said. "I'm trying not to think about that yet. Besides, I happen to know of a perfectly good university just down the road from here. Their science department has an excellent reputation."

"Not to mention the fact that children of employees get a discount on their tuition," Anna Mei said, grinning. "And students are allowed to live at home with their parents."

Mom laughed as she reached out for a hug. "Like I said, you never know."

Chapter Thirty-Three

Lucky Girl

On the day of the Science Quest state level competition, Anna Mei woke up early. Now that it was April, sunlight filtered into her bedroom in the mornings, growing stronger every day. All the spotty patches of snow had finally melted, and the air smelled like new grass and the first flowers of spring.

It was going to be a busy morning. The high school hosting the competition was two hours away, and they would need to leave by seven-thirty in order be there on time. Still, she decided to take a moment to snuggle with Cleo and think about the day ahead before she jumped into it.

She would be nervous competing against all the other teams—there was no question about that. But ever since helping Westside take second place at regionals last month, she felt confident that she and Kai could hold their own when it came time to answer the judges' questions. It turned out that they made a pretty good team after all.

That would make a victory today a little bittersweet, she realized. If the team moved on to the final competition, held next month in Washington, D.C., Kai wouldn't be there. The project at the university was in its final stages, and Dr. Chen had accepted a three-month position in Toronto, Canada. In just two weeks the Chens would be moving on.

"I can't believe it," Anna Mei said when Kai had told her about their plans. "I mean, I knew you would have to leave eventually, but now that you're really going, I just . . . it won't be the same without you, that's all."

"This will be different for me, also," Kai said. "I will not attend a regular school, since it is almost time for summer vacation. Instead I will go to a special summer camp for accelerated students. It should be a very interesting experience."

She hoped it would be. No matter how many times Kai insisted that it didn't bother him to change schools so often, she couldn't help feeling sorry for him. She told him that if his family ever ended up back in the United States, they should come and visit.

"Toronto is not so far from here," he pointed out. "Only a drive of six hours."

She nodded. "That's true. You could come back for a weekend, or maybe we could visit you there. You could show us around the city."

Now as Anna Mei pushed back the covers, she thought of how for many months, all she'd wanted was for the Chens to leave town. Then she could go back to thinking of herself as being just like everyone else—a thirteen-year-old girl in small-town America, living with her family and hanging out with her friends.

But she wasn't *just* like everyone else. She was a thirteen-year-old Chinese-American girl, living in a multi-cultural family and hanging out with kids from all different backgrounds. And that wasn't something to worry about—it was something to celebrate.

After finding an empty space in the school parking lot, the Andersons braved the crowded hallways, watching for signs that would lead them to Westside's designated space. The gym and cafetcria were bursting at the seams with display tables, all loaded with colorful projects, some of them whirring, buzzing and flashing.

"Anna Mei!" someone called, and she turned to see Miss Haynes waving her over to a spot in the gym. Kai was there, too, wearing his team shirt. His father had driven the family in their rented car, and now he and Kai's mother were already in the auditorium, waiting for the competition to begin. After helping Anna Mei set up her display board and her five sample plants, her parents went to join them.

"What's that?" Anna Mei asked, noticing another potted plant sitting in front of Kai's display board. "Did you add something new to your project?"

He shook his head and gave her that now-familiar half-smile. "It's a bamboo plant," he said. "My mother wanted us to have it for luck. But she said I am to remind you that you are already a very lucky girl."

There was no doubt about that, Anna Mei realized. Even with all the butterflies in her stomach, there was no other place she'd rather be.

"Your mother is right," she said, smiling, "I *am* lucky. But maybe we'd better go over some of these questions one more time—just in case."

Chapter Thirty-Four

An "Interesting Cultural Experience"

It was funny—after so many months of preparation, the actual competition flew by in what seemed like just a few minutes.

Later Anna Mei remembered explaining her project to the judges who came around with their clipboards, making notes as she talked. She remembered standing on the stage with the rest of her team, and taking turns with Kai as they answered questions about earth science. Looking out at the auditorium she'd seen her parents sitting with the Chens, all of them smiling in silent encouragement. Danny, Zandra, and Luis were there, too—Mr. Gallagher had volunteered to drive them after they'd insisted on coming to cheer for their fellow Westsiders.

When the judging was over their team had won an honorable mention trophy. Miss Haynes, bursting with pride, told them what an amazing accomplishment it was to finish in the top ten out of all the teams in Michigan. And Anna Mei and Kai had both won blue ribbons for their individual projects. Her father took about a million pictures of them with their awards, and Mrs. Chen's smile as she hugged her son practically lit up the whole auditorium.

Everyone had been too preoccupied to think about food during the event—with the possible exception of Danny, of course. As they headed for the parking lot he suggested that they all meet at a pizza parlor he'd seen at the highway exit.

"I hope you're not too disappointed about missing out on nationals, Anna Mei," her father said, as they followed the line of cars pulling out of the school driveway. "You really did a great job today—your mom and I are so proud of you."

"And we have something else to talk about," her mother said. "It's something we hope you'll think is pretty exciting, too."

She explained that while they were sitting together in the auditorium, the Chens invited the Andersons to visit them in Beijing. They could go anytime in August, after the Chens returned home from Toronto.

"Your dad and I would love to make the trip," Mom added. "We always said we wanted to go back some day, and this invitation seems like a perfect opportunity. It's just that . . . well, we weren't sure how *you'd* feel about it, Anna Mei. We don't want to pressure you in any way—if you don't want to go, then we just won't."

At first Anna Mei was too surprised to answer. She stared out the car window, watching the trees whiz by and wondering why everything was moving so fast—maybe *too* fast.

She thought again of the pictures in her social studies book, taken in the beautiful and mysterious country where she was born. She remembered the faces of the people, people who looked liked her, as they lived and worked and raised their families.

"Would we stay in Beijing the whole time?" she asked, suddenly thinking of the picture she kept on her dresser. It showed her as a baby, cradled in the arms of her new American parents as they stood on the steps of the orphanage. "Or would we go to Yiyang, too?"

"Only if you want to," Dad answered.

Did she want to?

How would it feel to actually visit the part of China where I was born? she wondered. *And what about seeing the orphanage where Mom and Dad first met me?* Thinking about it sent a shiver of excitement through her. She could picture getting ready to go—passports, airline tickets, and of course, a notebook so she could write everything down.

"I think we should go," she said finally, and saying the words out loud made her feel even more sure. It would be an amazing trip—maybe even the trip of a lifetime.

✳

The restaurant was pretty crowded, so they had to split up—the five adults at one table and five kids at the other. Luckily there was a pizza and salad bar, which meant they didn't have to wait for food.

After they'd filled their plates and sat down again, Anna Mei told her friends about the Chens' invitation.

"That sounds amazing!" Zandra said. "I'm definitely jealous. You'll have to tell me every single detail when you get back."

"And be sure to take pictures," Luis suggested. "We have a whole album from our trip to Mexico."

Kai nodded. "There are many beautiful sights in China. I am sure you will find it to be—"

"—a very interesting cultural experience!" Anna Mei finished for him, and everyone laughed, including Kai.

"It's funny," Zandra said. "I remember how upset you were when Kai first came to Westside."

"That's true," Anna Mei admitted, realizing how much things had changed since then. And with this trip to China in her future, there were sure to be a lot more changes ahead. "I guess I just didn't recognize a good thing when I saw it."

"That's okay, Cartoon Girl," Danny told her, his smile as bright as his blue eyes. "You know what they say about blessings—sometimes they come in disguise."

The moment he said it, she knew it was true. Her life was filled with blessings—some of them smiling brightly, others hiding behind a fake nose and black plastic glasses. But from now on, no matter how they came into her life, she would try to recognize them, and be grateful.

Carol A. Grund first introduced the character Anna Mei Anderson in *Anna Mei, Cartoon Girl* (Pauline Books & Media, 2010). The enthusiastic response to that story inspired the further adventures of Anna Mei and her friends in *Anna Mei, Escape Artist* and *Anna Mei, Blessing in Disguise* (both from Pauline Books & Media, 2011). Carol's stories and poems have appeared in children's magazines and book anthologies, including *Ladybug, Ladybug* (Carus Publishing), *Friend 2 Friend, Celebrate the Season* and *Family Matters* (all from Pauline Books & Media). She has also contributed to several *Chicken Soup for the Soul* collections. Find more about Carol—plus a special *Anna Mei* site—at CarolAGrund.com.

Book Guides

Investigating Anna Mei

Anna Mei, *Cartoon Girl*

First Impressions

1. What is Anna Mei's first impression of Danny? How does she feel at first about the Ponytail Club girls?
2. What worries does Anna Mei have on her first day at Elmwood?
3. Have you ever been "the new kid" somewhere? What were your concerns? How did things turn out?

Nicknames

1. Why does Danny call Anna Mei "Cartoon Girl"?
2. Why do you think this bothers Anna Mei so much?
3. What is the difference between name-calling and giving someone a nickname?
4. Do you have a nickname? Who gave it to you, and why?

Blending In

1. Why does Anna Mei have a hard time blending in?
2. What does Anna Mei do (or not do) to try to fit in?
3. Are there times when you would rather blend in than stand out? Why do you feel that way?
4. Why is it important to be yourself and not pretend to be someone else?

Making Friends

1. Although Anna Mei doesn't notice at first, in what ways does Danny behave like a real friend?
2. What makes Anna Mei change her mind about Danny?
3. Have you ever realized you were wrong about someone? What did that experience teach you about getting to know people?

White Lie

1. Is Anna Mei's friendship with the Ponytails dishonest? Why, or why not?
2. Why does Anna Mei lie and say that her parents can't help at the Fall Follies?
3. What happens when Mr. Anderson discovers her lie?
4. Have you ever been caught in a lie? How did it make you feel?
5. Why is telling the truth always the best option?

Fall Follies

1. How does Anna Mei hurt Danny's feelings?
2. If Anna Mei had been honest with the Ponytails about her friendship with Danny, what might she have said?
3. Do you act differently in front of different people? Why?
4. How do you feel when your friends meet your parents?

Heritage Report

1. Why does the heritage report cause Anna Mei so much stress?
2. Is a person's heritage important? Why or why not?

3. What is the significance of Anna Mei's name?
4. Why is her name an important part of who she is?

Starting Over

1. What do you know about the *real* Anna Mei?
2. There have been many changes in Anna Mei's life since the move, but what things have remained the same?
3. Why is Danny's Irish blessing so comforting for Anna Mei?
4. Some changes are exciting and others can make us feel sad or afraid. What changes have you found exciting? When you are sad or fearful about a change in your life, what brings you comfort?

Anna Mei, Escape Artist

Remember When?

1. Why is Anna Mei so excited to receive her yearbook?
2. Why was it surprising to see Anna Mei in a picture with Zoey, Rachel, and Amber?
3. Have you ever looked at your parents' old yearbooks or photo albums? How do your parents

react when they see something from when they were younger?

4. Think about your life a year ago. What has changed? What has remained the same? What have you learned about yourself?

Summer Plans

1. What would Danny's ideal summer break be like?
2. How is it different from Anna Mei's? How is it the same?
3. What would your ideal summer break be like? What was the best summer you ever had? What made it the best?

Babysitting

1. How does Anna Mei feel about babysitting her cousin, Emily?
2. What activities do both Anna Mei and Emily enjoy (perhaps in different ways)?
3. What qualities does a good babysitter have?
4. What do you enjoy doing with younger children in your family or neighborhood?

Priorities

1. Anna Mei casually cancels plans with her mom several times. Does she have good reasons when she does this?

2. How does Anna Mei's mom feel when this happens?
3. Has anyone canceled plans with you before? How did that make you feel?
4. How do you show friends and family that you care about them?

Not Quite Right

1. What events and habits make Anna Mei suspect that something is going on with Danny's family?
2. How does Anna Mei bring up her suspicions to Danny?
3. What would have been a better way for Anna Mei to tell Danny what was bothering her?
4. Have you ever been suspicious of someone's behavior? How did you deal with your suspicions?

Family Life

1. How is Zandra's home different from Anna Mei's?
2. Which one is more like your home? How so?
3. Have you ever spent the night at a friend's house? How was it similar to your house? How was it different?
4. Can you remember a time when you felt good just to be home?

Detective Work

1. There are several clues throughout the book that hint at what is going on with Danny's family. What are these clues?
2. Why do you think Anna Mei doesn't notice them?
3. Is there a difference between lying and keeping silent about the truth? Explain your reasoning.
4. Do you think Danny was wrong to keep the truth from Anna Mei? Why or why not?

Real Friendship

1. What is Anna Mei's definition of real friendship in Chapter Nineteen?
2. Why does this definition cause her to question her friendship with Danny?
3. How does her definition change by the end of the book?
4. How would you define real friendship?
5. How do you try to live up to that definition with your friends?

Thoughtless

1. Anna Mei is so caught up in her own feelings that she isn't able to imagine Danny's perspective. What misunderstandings does she have about the situation?

2. Why does she believe these things?

3. Why is it important to try to understand other perspectives?

4. What do you do when you have a misunderstanding with someone?

Being There

1. How did Anna Mei, without even knowing it, help Danny deal with his mother's illness?

2. What does the term "escape artist" mean?

3. How is Danny an escape artist? How is Anna Mei an escape artist?

4. Why is trying to escape from problems not the best solution?

5. What are some ways to be a good friend to someone who is having a difficult time?

Anna Mei, Blessing in Disguise

Traditions

1. What do Anna Mei and her friends and family do to celebrate Halloween?

2. How has Halloween changed for you as you've gotten older?

3. Are there some traditions that you used to love, but now find silly?

    4. What traditions do you think you'll never outgrow?

Balancing Act

1. Anna Mei quickly finds 7th grade to be challenging. What in particular does she have difficulty with?
2. What advice does Danny give her when she's tired?
3. How do you relax when you feel stressed out?
4. What's your strategy for balancing school, sports, friends, and extra-curricular activities?

Expectations

1. What does Anna Mei expect Kai to be like before she meets him? What is Kai actually like? How does this make Anna Mei feel?
2. What did Kai expect Anna Mei to be like and how did she surprise him?
3. Think about a time when you expected one thing and were surprised by reality. What were you expecting? What really happened? How did that make you feel?

Mixed Motives

1. Why does Kai join the Science Club and choose the earth science team?
2. What is Kai angry about?

3. How do your parents influence your participation in different activities?

4. Have you ever done something because someone else expected you to even if you didn't really want to? How did you end up feeling about that activity?

New Friends

1. What do Mr. and Mrs. Anderson do to welcome the Chens to their community?

2. Why do the Andersons want to get to know the Chens better and have them be a part of Anna Mei's life in particular?

3. What are some things you could do to welcome a new student or neighbor?

Sharing Faith

1. Why do the Chens look uncomfortable when Mr. Anderson says a prayer at Thanksgiving dinner?

2. What do you know about other religions?

3. Have you ever talked with friends about your beliefs or asked them about theirs?

Exploring Cultures

1. How does Luis blend his Mexican culture with his American culture?

2. Why does Anna Mei have a hard time identifying with her Chinese roots?

3. Where does your family's heritage come from?
4. How connected do you feel to your heritage?
5. Are there any cultural traditions that you and your family have preserved?

Over the Top

1. Why does Anna Mei become so angry during dinner with the Chens at the Jade Garden?
2. What does she do about it afterward?
3. Have you ever said something when you were upset that you later regretted?
4. How did you wish you would have handled the situation?
5. What did you do to make amends?

Putting Others First

1. Why does Anna Mei decide to quit the Science Club?
2. Why does Kai decide to quit the Science Club?
3. In your opinion, who do you think had the better reason for quitting? Why do you think that?
4. Have you ever given up something for the good of someone else? How did that make you feel?

Blessing in Disguise

1. What does the phrase "blessing in disguise" mean?

2. What different things would Kai, Anna Mei, and Mrs. Chen consider blessings in disguise?
3. What in your life has turned out to be a blessing in disguise?
4. Is there anything you can think of in your life that might be in disguise right now, waiting to be recognized as a blessing?

Anna Mei Series

Moving

Both Anna Mei and Kai move to Michigan. Think about how each one deals with the move and adjusts to changes. How are they the same? How are they different?

Jumping to Conclusions

Anna Mei has a habit of judging people before getting to know them. Throughout the series, who does she misjudge? What does she first think about them, and what does she end up thinking about them? Does it seem to you that Anna Mei learns from her mistakes or not?

Losing Touch

Describe Anna Mei's relationship with Lauren. What do you think will happen with their friendship? Why is it difficult to have a friend who lives far away? What are some ways to stay in touch?

Looking for Clues

Authors know what is going on in a character's life long before the reader finds out. Look back at Danny in *Cartoon Girl*. Are there any clues about his mother's illness? Knowing now what was going on with his mom at that time, how can we better explain some of his early interactions with Anna Mei?

Adoption

How has Anna Mei shown that she's grown more comfortable with her adoption?

How does Anna Mei's Chinese heritage affect her life in *Cartoon Girl* compared with *Blessing in Disguise*. What causes this change?

Without any new facts, how does Anna Mei come to understand and appreciate her birth mother more throughout the series?

Messages

What messages is Carol A. Grund trying to convey in each individual book?

What is the overall message that the books work together to convey?

A Catholic Place for Kids

A JClub Catholic Book Fair is more than just a school fundraiser. It is a multimedia experience for kids and a resource for schools to enhance existing curriculum. It's also easy; the program includes everything schools need to run a successful Catholic book fair. JClubCatholic.org includes educational and fun content, as well as information and resources for teachers and parents.

Email us at **JClub@paulinemedia.com** for more information or for a for FREE introductory kit.

www.jclubcatholic.org

"This was a great way for some of the children and families to acquaint themselves with a selection of Catholic books." — *Mary, IL*

"Just do it! This is an easy way to get some good material into the hands of the students." — *Julie, MO*

Who are the Daughters of St. Paul?

We are Catholic sisters. Our mission is to be like Saint Paul and tell everyone about Jesus! There are so many ways for people to communicate with each other. We want to use all of them so everyone will know how much God loves us. We do this by printing books (you're holding one!), making radio shows, singing, helping people at our bookstores, using the Internet, and in many other ways.

Visit our Web site at www.pauline.org

BOOKS & MEDIA

The Daughters of St. Paul operate book and media centers at the following addresses. Visit, call or write the one nearest you today, or find us on the World Wide Web, www.pauline.org

CALIFORNIA
3908 Sepulveda Blvd, Culver City, CA 90230 — 310-397-8676
935 Brewster Avenue, Redwood City, CA 94063 — 650-369-4230
5945 Balboa Avenue, San Diego, CA 92111 — 858-565-9181

FLORIDA
145 S.W. 107th Avenue, Miami, FL 33174 — 305-559-6715

HAWAII
1143 Bishop Street, Honolulu, HI 96813 — 808-521-2731

Neighbor Islands call: — 866-521-2731

ILLINOIS
172 North Michigan Avenue, Chicago, IL 60601 — 312-346-4228

LOUISIANA
4403 Veterans Memorial Blvd, Metairie, LA 70006 — 504-887-7631

MASSACHUSETTS
885 Providence Hwy, Dedham, MA 02026 — 781-326-5385

MISSOURI
9804 Watson Road, St. Louis, MO 63126 — 314-965-3512

NEW JERSEY
561 U.S. Route 1, Wick Plaza, Edison, NJ 08817 — 732-572-1200

NEW YORK
64 West 38th Street, New York, NY 10018 — 212-754-1110

PENNSYLVANIA
Philadelphia—relocating — 215-969-5068

SOUTH CAROLINA
243 King Street, Charleston, SC 29401 — 843-577-0175

VIRGINIA
1025 King Street, Alexandria, VA 22314 — 703-549-3806

CANADA
3022 Dufferin Street, Toronto, ON M6B 3T5 — 416-781-9131